ONE

From a glossy black and white photograph in a d   e
tingling electricity, the fluttering, deep within her i
would, to her, become a lifelong obsession stared :
a 2-inch by 2-inch photograph on the front cover (
crime paperback on a dusty pine shelf, sharing its s|
sized pictures of men such as Charles Manson, Ted
"20ᵗʰ CENTURY KILLERS" Read the bold headlin   catching red lettering,

with the sub-heading "The most evil men of the last 100 years".
Charlie, an accomplished thief, or at least a skilled shoplifter, immediately deciding that
she had to own the book, silently slipped the battered volume into her equally worn
rucksack and strode calmly from the store slowly, absently glancing at the covers of
novels as she left, as though still browsing. The middle-aged woman behind the till was
distracted, talking to another customer about her favourite Bernard Cornwell novels, so
deeply engrossed that Charlie's presence in the store did not seem to have even been
noticed, let alone acknowledged.
Charlie's attraction to the rugged, rough-looking man on the front cover of her stolen
book was baffling, even to herself. Whilst other girls at the various schools that Charlie
was regularly expelled from fawned over members of the latest manufactured boy bands,
or actors from current high school-oriented movies, a grainy photograph of a man who
had undoubtedly committed unspeakable crimes against other human beings was causing
Charlie's heart to hammer against the walls of her chest. She had always been impulsive,
but to steal a book because she found the man in a photograph on the cover attractive
was a brand-new experience for her.
She hurriedly walked the mile and a half to her place of sanctuary, West Dalton
Cemetery. The Cemetery, a large, well-kept burial ground just outside the town centre,
was not a conventional hangout for a thirteen-year-old girl, however, for a loner who
would usually become irritable after more than ten minutes in the presence of another
person, it was the best place to hide, to be in the company of her own thoughts, an area
with minimal chance of human contact, especially other kids. The occasional adults that
would solemnly lope by would either not notice her presence at all, wrapped up in their
own personal mourning, or sometimes they would glance briefly in her direction, offering
a tight-lipped smile.
*Of course, this poor girl has lost a loved one. We often see her sitting here. Poor soul, to learn of death at
such a young age. I wonder who she has lost? A parent? grandparent? Oh, I hope not a sibling. Better to
simply leave her alone.*
This was *her* place. No voices, no sound at all but for the wind whistling through the
trees, blowing between the headstones. The names on the stones, she thought, were once
walking, breathing people with families, homes, jobs. Once happy, falling in love,
enjoying holidays in the sun, thinking that it would all never end. Now these folk were
eternally silent. The best kind of company.
Just me and the dead here. These people at least don't try to force me into social contact.
Charlie had settled on the bench, *her* bench, and taken several deep breaths, basking in
the silence, calming her thoughts, her often dark thoughts. She slowly pulled out the
stolen book from her bag and stared once again upon the image that had snared her.
Sidney Taylor's police mugshot showed a dark, brooding figure with combed-back raven
coloured hair and a face that had clearly not seen a razor for two or three days. He was
young, perhaps mid-twenties, and could have been handsome less for the facial scars,
unkempt appearance and shark-like, soulless expression.

Charlie sipped at a half bottle of dark rum as she read, stolen of course, from the local supermarket, and puffed away at a cigarette from the packet she had taken from the bedroom of her current foster parents. They were paid more than enough for tolerating her presence anyhow, she decided, and they certainly weren't in it for the love.

As she drank, she read and re read the pages describing Taylor. His chapter was short, much shorter than the chapters on Manson or Bundy, despite his face sharing the glory of the front cover with theirs. Very little was mentioned about his background, but the limited information within the chapter caused her attraction to him to deepen more intensely with every word that she read. He, like she, was an orphan raised in the care system, growing up committing petty crimes and being repeatedly forced to relocate, being ejected from both schools and homes. From the age of fourteen, he seemed to disappear from the face of the planet until his re-emergence with an arrest and incarceration at twenty-four years old in the year 1993 for severely beating a biker in a bar fight. Upon his release, Taylor vanished again, only catching the interest of the authorities two years later when he was the target of a police manhunt after eighteen bodies, most of which had decomposed for periods between one year and eighteen months, were discovered by a dog walker in the cellar of an abandoned house thought to have been previously inhabited by a male who matched the description of the ex-convict named Sidney Taylor. He had very few associates, but there had been reports to police around the time of the deaths of the victims of a rugged-looking, heavily built man lurking around the old farm buildings by a few nervous trekkers and dog walkers that had been passing by. Still, why a dog walker had taken his dog into the cellar of an abandoned farmhouse was left for readers to ponder.

Sid Taylor was never apprehended for the crimes. He was, however, found.

Two months into the nationwide search, four bodies were found in a top floor flat rented by a barmaid named Nicola Donovan, after neighbours reported the sounds of screaming, and what sounded to be a violent struggle, coming from within the flat above their heads. The police arrived at what one Officer later described as a "compressed war zone. Everything smashed to pieces. Blood and bodies everywhere."

One body, a female who was later discovered to be Donovan, had been beaten and strangled to death. The other three were adult males. Two of them were bikers, known by police to be members of the Blackhearts Motorcycle Club, one chapter of which was a gang thought to be running Class A drugs and prostitution in the area. These men had been stabbed through the chest and neck numerous times in what was clearly a frenzied attack. The other male had been subjected to unthinkable torture. He had been beaten, with bruising and lacerations covering most of his body, and worse, the flesh on his face had been burned off right down to the bone by what was believed to be a blowtorch. The man with no face was Sidney Taylor.

A large hunting knife was discovered, covered in Taylor's fingerprints. Forensics reports determined that the two Bikers had been stabbed to death by Taylor, whereas Donovan had been strangled by a fifth person whom had never been apprehended. The working hypothesis of the police was that Taylor had been shacked up with Nicola Donovan in the small flat, when his enemies finally came knocking. The door had been kicked in, and several males had entered the flat in search of the fugitive. A struggle had ensued, with Taylor succeeding in stabbing to death two of his attackers. The remaining thugs had managed to beat, and eventually hold down, the struggling killer, whilst one of their number began to work on his face with the blowtorch. It was thought that Donovan, although she was not a target as such, was beaten and eventually strangled purely because she was in the way, and also due to the fact that a witness that could describe any of the home invaders in court, should the matter go to trial. Sidney Taylor had died in the winter of 1996, when the young Charlie had been but four years old.

Why the Blackhearts had targeted Sid Taylor in such a brutal way that day had never been established. Several gang members had been questioned as part of the investigation, however, due to their strict code of silence when dealing with the authorities, nobody had spoken a word. None of the known gang members brought in for questioning matched any of the finger or foot prints found at the scene, and subsequently they were all released due to lack of evidence. Taylor was a mystery. Why had he killed his victims? Why, and how, did he make an enemy of the Blackhearts? Why was he living with a barmaid in a run-down flat in a seedy part of a seedy town? Where did he go during his long disappearances?

His victims had all been male, aged between thirty-one and fifty-seven years old. They varied in social class, background and profession. Two of them had been convicted paedophiles, one of them a Solicitor, two builders, and even one priest. Nothing had linked the victims to Taylor, or even to each other. None of the bodies had been sexually assaulted, no trophies were taken. They had simply been stabbed repeatedly, dragged down the cellar stairs, then covered with lime and gravel, then topped with car air fresheners. Why or how Taylor had managed to lure them to the abandoned house in which he was squatting was unknown, but it appeared that they had all met their ends within those walls. The glossy centre pages within the book displayed a black and white picture of the crime scene. An old two storey farmhouse, disused, dilapidated, isolated. *Nobody could hear the screams.*

Clearly the photograph had been taken some time after the police had lost all interest in the old building as a crime scene. Like before, it looked abandoned, unwanted, unloved. A single, torn strand of police crime scene tape lay across the patchy grass to the front of the property; the only sign that the ignored house had once been the centre of all attention. The front page of the tabloids. Now, again, forgotten.

Beneath the photograph read the caption "House of horrors".

That's original.

Taking another sip of rum and rinsing it around her teeth like mouthwash, Charlie absently watched as a spider walked slowly across the armrest of the aged wood bench, whilst she pondered on how Sid Taylor had survived during his time spent living off the grid. He had seemingly used the "House of horrors" as a shelter, at least for a time, as the police did discover a sleeping bag and food waste within, but how did he eat? Where did the money come from? Did he rob his victims? Likely. But how did he, especially with his appearance, convince the men to follow him to an isolated, creepy old shell of a building far from where anyone could hear any cries for help?

Charlie placed her open hand in front of the spider and watched it crawl onto her palm. She lifted it and stared expressionlessly as it dropped down from her hand on its web like a bungee jumper, lowering itself to her knees below. She sipped at her bottle, tasting the molasses of the rum, feeling the welcome numbness and warmth as the alcohol began to slowly enter her bloodstream. The foster parents would smell the booze, that was for sure. They would shout a little, obviously through the fear of social services taking away their right to foster. Fuck them. Anyone that pretended to care for a child just to earn a little cash was beneath contempt.

If only she could figure out how Sid had survived whilst living off the grid. With that knowledge, she could disappear as he had, live alone with the darkness, forsaking humanity and no longer having the need to deal with the mindless, shambling droves of media obsessed sheep, harassing her for straying away from the flock.

That's how Sid saw them, for sure. Like cattle. He hated them. He would have liked me, though. He would have taken me under his wing, protected me.

Charlie swung up her feet onto the bench, and using her rucksack as a pillow, laid back and stared at the clouds. She lit another cigarette, closing her eyes and drawing deeply, inhaling the poisonous smoke.

Don't wait up, I won't be back til late. If I come back tonight.

For Charlie, the discovery of Sid Taylor had illuminated her life, given her a new lease of life, like a beacon in the darkness. The long days spent drinking alone in cemeteries no longer seemed so lonely. She always somehow felt that he was there *with her*, watching over her, protecting her. Of course, she knew even at her young age that this was all simply a fantasy, but she somehow no longer felt alone in the world. She had finally found another person, albeit dead, that she could relate to.

She bought or stole as many books on Taylor as she could, collected newspaper articles from archives, soaking up as much information on the deceased serial killer as was possible for her to access. The surviving photographs of him were few in number; two childhood pictures from the orphanage, a small handful of photographs of him with Nicola Donovan along with a few that Donovan had taken of him alone. Charlie treasured these pictures of the solemn killer with the pained face. Forensic Psychologists claimed Taylor to be a psychopath incapable of feelings for others, that his ice-cold heart had been forged through the years in the orphanage, with no family or even friends that could be traced, then he was further hardened in the years drifting through towns sleeping rough and his time behind bars, and that his relationship with Donovan was not for love or companionship, but rather through necessity. The killer with the stone heart had faked affection towards her, in order to use her abode as a hideout, as a shelter both from his enemies and from the law, and had thus indirectly caused her death.

Charlie disagreed.

You Psychologists don't know him like I do. He's a subject that you studied, perhaps for a week or so. I'm a fucking subject matter expert on Sid Taylor.

She truly believed, in her young heart, that Sid had been overwhelmed by the love that Nicola Donovan showed him, tenderness that he had experienced from no other person in his relatively short life, and that she had melted that heart of ice of his. How they had met was not certain, however, it was thought that Taylor had been renting a room at the time they met, using a false name, and working various cash-in-hand jobs in the area. The regular patrons of the bar in which Nicola worked had later swore that Sid had often sat alone at the bar sipping bottles of beer, talking to the young barmaid who had appeared to take a shine to the rough-looking, scarred, silent man whose path every other regular in the bar feared to cross, let alone try to speak to him. One bouncer at the bar, however, claimed to like having Sid around, as nobody would dare start any trouble in Donovan's presence whilst Sid Taylor, her friend, drank at the bar.

The more Charlie read and the more TV documentaries that she watched, the more of a mystery Sidney Taylor became. More knowledge created even more unanswered questions. And whilst most girls in their early teens eventually grew out of their childhood crushes, or at least found new ones, Charlie's fascination with her only love grew with her. She went from foster home to foster home, then eventually on to the Young Offender's Institute, thinking of him. Every street that she walked, every cemetery that she drank in, every bar that she frequented, right through to adulthood, thinking of Sid. Long dead Sid, whose last breath was sucked through burnt lips a year before Charlie's first day at school. Sid, the enigmatic murderer that she could never possibly meet. Sid, the only man that she had ever loved. Sure, there had been men. Women, too. As she grew older, social contact repulsed her slightly less as her sexual urges developed, and she occasionally would enjoy a drink or two with a good-looking guy or girl in a bar. If she found them both attractive *and* interesting, she may well end up fucking them. But if they started to ask for a date, then the new friendship would be invariably over. Charlie didn't date. That was a modern mating ritual for civilised people seeking a long-term relationship, or worse. "Dating" was a farce, something that belonged in mediocre American romantic comedy movies. Of course, Charlie had slept with a small handful of people on more than one occasion, with some partners she had even met up with for sex on regular occasions for several weeks; as long as they understood that sex was all it was, and maybe a few drinks, or a joint or a line of coke here and there, that was fine. Having some fun with another person could be good; it was when the text messages asking how she was or what she was up to began to appear on her phone would be the time that all connections would be cut.

A relationship with another, be they male or female, could never work anyhow. Not only was Charlie a free spirit and a loner at heart, but who would ever understand a person with a fixation on a man who had been dead for almost 25 years? Especially when that man had been a multiple murderer? And who could ever live in the shadow of this man, playing second best? The kind of man who would be content to play second fiddle to a corpse was by no means the kind of man that Charlie could ever respect; besides, the thought of commitment to another person had always been sickening to her. Seeing couples walking around garden centres looking at shades of wood stain was as depressing to Charlie as movies about Auschwitz. Just not entertainment.

One-night flings were more her thing. She loved to experiment sexually, the experiments often involving pain, inflicted by her, against the other. Charlie had come to realise from an early age that she was a sadist that loved to hear the screams of others and know that she was the cause of it. Unfortunately, to enjoy the indulgence of this side of her persona meant that she was forced to forsake another side of herself; the self-isolating loner. The torture of other people had the unfortunate side-effect of having to enter into close proximity with another person.

This desire for sexual contact eventually led Charlie's path to cross with the path of one Ashton Drake. She had taken some bar work in a rock bar close to the railway station on the edge of town, a bar that, despite the rumbles from the occasional train drowning out the sound of the classic heavy rock music, suited her perfectly. Its location, away from the town centre, kept away the mainstream clubbers, and the almost underground atmosphere of the place attracted very particular crowds. There was firstly the alternative crowd, who to Charlie were quite a mixed bag. The girls, she thought, were sometimes hot, but the guys, not so much. Men with facial piercings and long fringes dyed in bizarre colours hanging over their eyes never quite caught her attention. Although her own sense of style was quite alternative, with her combat boots, multiple tattoos and dark clothing, some of the types of men that this look typically tended to attract were really not her type. Another crowd that haunted *JACK THE RIPPERS* was much more fuckable, in Charlie's opinion, the tattooed rocker type. *JACK's* did attract a considerable number of muscular biker-looking types, attracted by the music, by the lack of fake, conventional types, and by the lure of the rock chicks within.

These guys are the real men. They don't follow the crowd, and yet they're not effeminate fucking emos either.

Charlie was opening a bottle of dry cider for a red-haired girl with a ridiculous-looking central nose piercing that, along with the hair colour, reminded Charlie of a Highland cow, when she saw, sitting alone with a bottle of Budweiser, a heavily-built, intense looking man staring directly ahead at the rows of spirits behind the bar. His face, bearded and covered in scars, was set in a stony expression of deep concentration.

Oh my fucking god, it's him. Sid is here.

She stared for several seconds at the stranger, allowing the vision to soak into her brain. Was it an illusion? Or a ghost? His hair is cropped short now, and he's grown his beard a little. He looks different.

That's because it's not Sid. Get a grip, girl. It's just a guy. A random guy.

"Hey, can I have my drink?"

The redhead. The redhead with the bull ringed nose.

"Yeah, sorry…"

The girl snatched her bottle of Thatchers without thanks, striding away with a childish sulk.

"You're welcome…" Charlie murmured absently as she walked slowly over towards the stranger. His plain white T-Shirt hugged his muscular frame closely, his skin was tanned, not fake tan, not sunbed tanned, but the uneven brown complexion of a man who had been working out in the heat, and like his face, his arms were knotted with numerous scars that intertwined with the tattoos. As she approached, his eyes didn't move, didn't acknowledge her. Whatever deep thought that this man was engaged in were clearly much more compelling than the barmaid in combat boots that crept slowly towards him.

"I've got a drink, thanks," He finally spoke, his eyes dropping from the spirit bottles down to the beer bottle in his fist. "I'll let you know when I need another." His accent had a twang, not quite English. European, perhaps.

Charlie glanced down at the beer.

"That American piss? You can hardly call that a drink."

At last, he looked up, making eye contact. He looked at her with a look that was both quizzical and mildly angry. His eyes were pale blue, intense, soul piercing.

"I prefer French beer. This place only serves piss like this."

"You're French?"

He laughed, staring down at the label on his bottle.

"I don't even know what I am anymore."

Charlie waited for a moment, expecting more of an explanation. When it didn't come, she moved swiftly on, changing the subject.

"Let me get you a real drink."

She reached for a bottle of Absinthe, then a dry Gin. The stranger watched calmly as she poured a shot of the green liquid, then a shot of the clear into glass and gave it a stir.

"This is called a London fog. I didn't add ice; I thought maybe you looked cold enough." She set the glass in front of him, and he glanced down at it, then back up at her face. He briefly looked her up and down, shrugged, then picked up the drink, giving it a small sniff.

"Fuck me man, I haven't poisoned you. Drink the damned thing. It's on me." She offered a small half smile, leaning down and resting on her elbows as she watched him.

"Why?"

"You're drinking alone, you look like something is on your mind, and I don't like talking to the emos and vampire wannabes in here. Drink up."

He looked around the room, as though he were noticing the other patrons within the bar for the first time, clearly attempting to suppress a small smile. He then tipped back his head and downed the greenish fluid in one. He slammed the glass down onto the bar, then slid it back towards Charlie with a dismissive push with the back of his hand.

"Gone. Happy now? Can I get back to my American piss?"

"What's your name?"

"Why?."

"My name's Charlie. Now tell me yours."

He glanced up, once again staring directly into her eyes with that burning stare. He held the gaze for three or four long seconds, then spoke.

"No."

His eyes then broke contact and he glanced down at his right hand, staring at a ring on his index finger, a thick silver piece bearing the face of a helmeted Samurai. His expression appeared haunted.

Charlie didn't know what to say. She smiled in spite of herself, despite the rejection. This man was interesting. An enigma. And he clearly wasn't all that interested in her. He wasn't interested *at all*.

That's so hot.

She left him alone with his Budweiser, walking away to serve a hipster-looking guy in a flat cap, tweed jacket and John Lennon spectacles.

"Hey, how are you? What ales do you have on tap?" He asked, his eyes on her cleavage.

Oh Christ. How long until he tells me that he's a fucking vegan?

Drake took small sips of his beer, swirling the frothy liquid around his tongue in a desperate attempt to draw out some flavour, to no avail. He glanced down at the label. The barmaid was right. The stuff really was piss. It tasted of soda water and certainly wasn't having the medicinal effect that he had hoped for. The Absinthe had been much better. Maybe he needed another.

This night spot had been the best option of a very bad bunch when he had weighed up his options, a fact that spoke volumes about this town. He certainly couldn't stomach any mindless, thumping dance music, nor could he bear to be in the company of equally moronic groups of short-skirted, high-heeled, intoxicated young twenty year old women with make-up that had apparently been laid on by a trainee plasterer, nor could he be around the amphetamine-fuelled young males with plucked eyebrows and fake tan, dancing poorly around them in an attempt to find a hole for their dick for the night. No, he certainly could not be in the presence of such people, not tonight, not without punching somebody. Or everybody.

The rock bar, *JACK THE RIPPER'S* would at least have tolerable music and a marginally less annoying populace. The other option would be to sit alone in the small room in the town centre that he had rented temporarily, alone with the demons and the memories. Seeing the faces, the shapes, in the darkness, Hearing the *voices*.

Whilst company was not something that he sought, or even wanted, the music and the alcohol would be a distraction; it would keep away the thoughts, and the voices. And, like always, remaining aware of his surroundings in a social context would keep his mind on matters other than the darkness.

Back in the day, the two of us would be looking for more than a bottle of Bud, Drakey. You're turning into my dad.

Frank's voice, forever guiding. Forever mocking.

It's not the same without you, though, Frankie.

Drake turned his gaze to his left, back towards the barmaid, who was rolling her eyes without humour as a hipster was clearly attempting to make a joke or cheap chat-up line. She had a round, firm behind, wrapped in her tight blue jeans, and a close-fitting black vest top showing firm, well-sized breasts. A silver chain hung around her neck, slightly thicker than one that a girl would normally wear. Like a man's chain. Her toned arms were completely covered in intricate tattoos, ravens, clouds, a winged Valkyrie. Beautiful, well shaded work. Her hair, jet black, was short at the back, the long fringe sloping down and hanging over one side of her face. She was certainly well formed. Hot, even. But company was not what he was seeking. Intoxication was what he needed right now, oblivion, to the point that he couldn't hear the demons in his head.

Hello Darkness, my old friend.

Besides, the barmaid was fucking annoying. He didn't need the company of an irritating woman, however attractive. He did, however, need another drink. And rescuing her from the hipster would be his good deed for the year.

"Hey!" He called, grabbing her attention. He waved his empty bottle.

The girl smiled as she approached, a small smile, forced.

"I'm thinking," he said thoughtfully, staring over her shoulder at the bottles behind the bar, "I need more Absinthe."

"You liked the London fog then? I knew you would. A good barmaid knows what a customer wants even better than he knows himself."

Drake ignored her attempt at conversation, nodding towards the Absinthe bottle. "Another London fog, and a bottle of IPA. Please."

The girl's smile dropped slightly as she turned her back to tend to his request.

You're being a prick, Drakey. She gave you a free drink. And you won't even tell her your name.

Drake, ignoring Frank's mocking voice, watched her silently pour the Gin, all attempts at conversation on her part seemingly abandoned.

Frankie, you were always the talkative one. Conversation was never my strong point.

Then you're going to become Celibate, my friend.

He sighed. Maybe some company for one night wouldn't hurt. If nothing else, it would be another distraction.

"My name's Ash." He said, almost begrudgingly.

Charlie looked up at him warily, the Gin bottle in one hand, his glass in the other.

"So now you want to talk? What changed?"

"I'm bored," he replied, "I thought you might entertain me. Juggle some bottles, do some fancy cocktail shit."

She smirked "You've seen the extent of my cocktail skills when I poured this," She said as she placed his drink before him, "I hope you're entertained."

Drake glanced around at the other faces in the bar. There were around twenty people in there, four sat around the bar, including himself, five on the dancefloor, with the rest sitting around the various tables and sofas. He pointed over at a blonde overweight girl with several ear and facial piercings who was speaking to the barman at the other side of the bar, whilst leaning forwards in an attempt be heard over the AC/DC track in the background.

"So… what is she going to order?"

"How the fuck would I know?"

Drake grinned "A good barmaid always knows what the customer wants better than they know themselves."

"I didn't say I was a *good* barmaid."

"Well, I'm guessing Jack and coke. She looks like a typical blasphemer who would ruin a good whisky with over sweetened chemical crap."

Charlie stared over at the girl.

"Nah, she's a German beer drinker. I'd say a Becks girl. Bottle of Becks."

"Okay, you're on, barmaid. Loser buys a drink."

"I bought the last one, you cheeky fucker."

The pair watched as the barman pulled a green beer bottle from the fridge and opened it. Becks.

Drake raised his eyebrows, "Very good. I'm impressed.

"She drinks Becks, but she *would* prefer a Spanish beer. A San Miguel. She just doesn't know it yet."

"This skill of yours is the most useless superpower I've ever heard of."

Charlie laughed. "And it's not even a real superpower. I've served that girl three times tonight already. With Becks."

Drake smiled absently, again staring off into space. Whatever troubling thoughts had haunted him previously in the evening were now returning. This man had clearly been through some rough times and it seemed that he hadn't quite left them behind.

"So, Ash….. What do you do for a living? You already now what I do. It's only fair." Charlie's desire to unravel the mystery of this man was causing her to cross social boundaries that she seldom had in the past. Small talk was not normally her speciality, and other than Sidney Taylor, never before had she been too overly interested in the background of anyone that she had met.

What do you do for a living? What kind of question is that? Come on Charlie, he must be bored of you already.

Drake continued staring at the spirit bottles over her shoulder, looking at them without seeing them. In his mind, he was elsewhere, a distant, dangerous land. With Frankie.

Get back to reality, Drakey. I'm right here in this bar with you. I'm always here.

"What do you think I do for a living?" He replied, his gaze again moving down to the Samurai ring on his clenched fist resting on the bar, the grimy bar that was coated in a fine film of stale beer and mixers that caused his hand to stick to it whenever he made contact.

Charlie looked him up and down. The scars, the thousand-yard stare, the troubled expression, the body rippled with muscle. Something dangerous, a profession that diced with death. Firefighter? Police? Military?

"You're a serial killer." She finally blurted out.

Drake's head snapped towards her. He stared at her hard for a moment, those intense eyes making her uncomfortable, yet simultaneously, somehow aroused.

"What?"

"You remind me of Sidney Taylor. So I said, you're a serial killer."

He dropped his gaze, exhaled, relaxed slightly.

"Sidney Taylor? Is that the guy who buried all those people in the farmhouse?"

"That's the one. He's adorable." Charlie turned and leaned back against the bar, looking up to the ceiling. She took a sip of her own drink, a dark rum on the rocks, and breathed deeply, "But he didn't exactly bury them. He just covered them with a little lime and gravel."

Drake stared at the girl. What a fucking oddball this one was. He and Frankie had met stranger folk on their travels, but strange she was nonetheless.

"Sid Taylor is adorable?" He laughed, "Maybe you and I will get on, after all."

Charlie was delighted to discover that Drake was more than willing to indulge her violent sexual urges. He was one of the more adventurous in the bedroom that she had encountered in the many long years of her numerous conquests. They had drank together for the remainder of her shift, their chat only disturbed by the fact that she was still required to pour drinks and open bottles for customers other than Drake and herself. The more alcohol that he drank, the more he seemed to relax and open up to her. They joked, spoke of music, her tattoos, their favourite drinks. Everything but each other's past. They flirted, mostly by insulting each other. She felt the muscles on his arm, and despite them feeling like steel, she joked, *Come on, don't you even work out? That's like the arm of a pre-pubescent boy.* He told her that she needed to diet, she told him that he should try a protein shake. This exchange of insults went on for some time, the two of them growing hornier with each line of abuse.

After her shift had ended, they retired to Drake's rented room in a large three storey house, a twenty-minute walk from *JACK's*, when, as soon as they closed the bedroom door, Charlie had surprised Drake by slapping him across the cheek and pushing him hard into the wall. She went to strike him again, but he was fast, very fast, despite the level of his intoxication, and before the slap could connect, he had caught her arm with both hands, span one hundred and eighty degrees, and thrown her over his shoulder, slamming her back onto the floor. The wind was knocked out of her, and before the shock could even register in her brain, he was upon her, pinning all her limbs, trapping her beneath him. She smiled lustfully, looking up at his eyes and his burning expression.

"I want to hurt you" She whispered.

"You can try." He replied, before leaning down and kissing her neck delicately.

"Let me tie you to the bed"

"No."

"Please…"

He ignored her, his lips moving down to her breasts. He nibbled at her nipples through her clothing, feeling them harden as he chewed, hearing her gasp. Having this psychotic bitch tie him up could either be a fantastic, erotic experience, or the death of him. Or even both.

Let her have her way, Drakey. You've fucked scarier girls than this one.

That's true, Frankie, but if some crazy bitch ever tried to slice me up whilst I was tied to a bed in the past, all I needed to do was call you from the next room. Where are you now?

When did you become such a pussy, Drakey?

She squirmed beneath him, struggling to free herself. His dick hardened beneath his jeans as he felt her writhing movements below.

"I want to hurt you…" She repeated, "Please let me play…"

Drake stood, releasing her, and pulled off his T-Shirt, tossing it to one side. Charlie climbed to her feet and pushed him by the shoulders back onto the bed. She unclipped his belt, unzipped his jeans and released his erect manhood from within.

Drake stared, allowing her to take control, breathing deeply as her mouth slowly moved down and enveloped his dick, her big green eyes never leaving his.

She's a stunner, Drakey. Enjoy her.

She sucked gently for a few moments, then removed her mouth.

"If you want this, Ash," She said softly, running one finger along her bottom lip suggestively, "Then you're going to have to let me tie you to the bed.."

Two hours later, as Drake lay on the bed, covered in bruises and bite marks, Charlie walked naked around the room, smoking a cigarette as she studied the sparse belongings within.

Drake was not amused at her filling his room with smoke and the stench of tobacco, but he said nothing. He watched as she snooped, opening his wardrobe, examining his belongings. What a nosy bitch.

A mirrored double oak wardrobe sat opposite the bed, with a chest of matching drawers against the wall to the right. There was a bedside cabinet to the left of the bed. Besides the clothes within the wardrobe and drawers, there was very little sign of life within the walls. Drake was clearly a very neat man, his clothes hanging neatly on hangers within the wardrobe; a black suit, a black military style jacket, some shirts, a couple of polo shirts, all ironed and hanging neatly with evenly spaced gaps between them.

On top of the chest of drawers sat a sheathed dagger and what looked like a fist-sized clear crystal skull, carved with symbols that appeared to be stained with faded brown paint. She glanced over to the bedside cabinet and noticed a small black book sitting beside a closed lock knife.

Why all the knives, Ash?

Charlie padded barefoot over to the bedside cabinet and picked up the book, a small black leather-bound thing. She opened it, seeing that it was a photo album. Of all Drake's sparse possessions, this was clearly one of his most cherished, sitting within arm's reach by his bed, beside the weapon that he clearly always felt that he needed to have close to hand . Did he have enemies? Was somebody out looking for him?

Oh fuck, Ash… If a bunch of bikers kick the door down and kill us both, when we get to hell, I'll certainly give you an eternity of torture.

The first photograph within the book showed two young, smiling men in military camouflage, in green berets with a circular cap badge that couldn't clearly be deciphered. One of the men was a younger, thinner, happier looking, clean shaven Ashton Drake. The other, a fair-haired youth who, Charlie judged from his arrogant expression, carried a cocky air of superiority.

Charlie glanced over at Ash, who was still laying on the bed, eyeing her suspiciously through the corner of his eye.

"Do you always go through other people's stuff? What the fuck are you doing?"

Ignoring him, Charlie glanced down at the tattoo on Ash's upper arm, a winged parachute, like a military parachutist's badge of sorts, she supposed. Above the parachute was a circular symbol, displaying within the circle what appeared to be a winged arm, holding a sword.

"You were a paratrooper?"

Drake broke his gaze away from hers, staring straight ahead, the vacant stare like the expression that he wore earlier in the evening in the bar returning again to his haunted face.

"Something like that." He replied.

"I used to fuck a Royal Marine. He didn't speak highly of paras."

"That's cute."

She looked down at the photo again, studying the two young men.

"I thought paras wore maroon berets?"

"Some do. British paras do. I wasn't in the British Army. I was a legionnaire."

A legionnaire. He had been in the French Foreign Legion. That explained some of the mysteries of Ashton Drake. It explained his accent, for certain. He was clearly an adventurer, a man that liked to challenge himself.

"Was?" Charlie looked up from the photo, "So now what? Where do you work?"

"Where do I work? Wherever the work is."

She flicked the page in the book, to the next photograph. The same two people, Ash and the unknown comrade, much younger, perhaps thirteen or fourteen, this time wearing white martial arts training suits, looking sweaty and dishevelled, arms around each other's shoulders, wearing black belts and proudly holding certificates. Young Ash looked proud and elated, his blonde companion wearing a smug expression.

"What is the black belt for? Which martial art, I mean?"

"In the photo? I don't remember. I hold a few black belts. Back when I chased belts in Asian martial arts. I trained seven days a week back then."

"Seven days a week? Did you even *have* a childhood?"

Drake scowled. Childhood. Not something that he wanted to remember.

Don't think about him, Drakey. He's dead and gone.

"So are you, Frankie," he mumbled, "But yet you're still here."

Charlie Looked up, hearing Drake mumble something incoherent.

"Huh?"

"Nothing."

She turned the page again. The same two men, older now, bearded, in baseball caps and shades, wearing black military body armour over desert tan coloured t-shirts, holding assault rifles. They were in some desert somewhere, standing in front of a huge SUV. Private military Contractors.

"You're a fucking mercenary?"

"I'm a lot of things." Drake then closed his eyes, clearly tiring of the interrogation. The sex had been good, a nice distraction, but this talkative woman was now outstaying her welcome.

Charlie continued to flick through the photographs. Every single one of them of Ash and his companion, with varying backdrops. Some more of them from their legionnaire days, some more of them as children and teenagers, in martial arts gear, boxing gear, pictures of them being awarded medals, being awarded belts. There was one of them both much younger, perhaps nine or ten, in clean white martial arts *Gis*, in white belts, standing with an older man a man in a black *Gi* with a black belt, his arms proudly around the two boys. His hair was prematurely grey, his face appearing much younger than the age that his hair suggested. Charlie guessed mid-thirties. A teacher, a sensei perhaps.

Ash's fairer companion was much larger than Ash, both in height and build, even as children. Ash was big enough, perhaps six foot three; his friend was clearly a giant, perhaps pushing on for six foot seven.

"Is this other guy your brother?"

"We weren't blood related," Drake replied, "But yes, he was my brother."

"Where is he now?"

"He's dead. I fucking killed him. Now shut up and let me sleep."

Charlie awoke alone in Drake's bed, with the sunlight throwing a beam across her naked breasts through a gap in the curtain. She could hear the scrubbing sound of teeth being brushed in the bathroom next door, and a tap running steadily. Perhaps it was time to leave now, before the miserable bastard came back in. She could shower back at home. Not only was he a moody bastard whose company, once he had received the sex that he had obviously wanted, was no joy, he had also claimed to have murdered his best friend. Surely, she thought, he had made it all up. He had said it just to shut her up. But then in that case, where *was* his friend? They were clearly joined at the hip, judging by the photographs that she had seen. Inseparable. Had they had a disagreement? A falling out? Maybe, but then why would he keep a set of photographs close by? Had he been killed in combat? Perhaps. Maybe Ash blamed himself. It would certainly explain his miserable face and his inability to hold a normal conversation. After a lifetime of avoiding most human contact and despising those who attempted to force it on her, Charlie had found herself for the first time being the one attempting to squeeze conversation from another. *Is that how I come across to other people? Like him? A miserable shit sitting there with a face like a blobfish, scowling at everyone?*

She stood, looking around for her clothes, deciding on leaving the house before he walked back into the room with his frown, when her eyes again caught sight of the crystal skull on top of the drawers. It appeared to stare at her, *willing* her to approach. The hypnotic, all-encompassing pull that she had experienced from the battered book in the second-hand store fifteen years previously, she now felt again from this fist-sized ornament. Forgetting her clothes, she walked around the bed and approached the skull. The symbols were simple, crude ones, but small and numerous, covering the entire surface. The silver chain that she wore around her neck began to feel as though it was heating up, as though someone had been holding it within a fire, causing a thin line of pain around her skin. Her arm instinctively raised and reached out for the skull, almost involuntarily, her hand wanting it, *needing* it, needing to feel the energy within… It was as though it called to her. Of course, she wasn't going to *steal* it, she grew out of that game years ago, and besides, she would only steal from shops, places that could *afford* it, but never from anyone's *home*, she wasn't going to *take* it, she just needed to feel the *energy* in her *palm…*

"Don't touch that!" Snapped Drake, now standing in the doorway with a clean red towel around his waist.

Charlie's hand snapped back, away from the skull.

"I wasn't going to take it, I…"

"Don't touch it!" He repeated, calmer this time. He stepped forwards and snatched up the skull angrily, opened the top drawer and dropped the thing inside, slamming it shut then staring intensely at her.

"Okay, okay!" She cried, stepping backwards towards the bed, "You really are a miserable cunt! I'll be leaving now."

Drake sighed.

She's right you know. Lighten up for fuck's sake. You'll be happier.

"I'm sorry, it's just…" He shook his head and sat down on the bed, next to where she stood. "Never mind. It's just…. Dangerous."

Charlie stared over at the drawer, the overwhelming urge to open it, grab the skull and run away slightly dampened by the fact that she was still naked. A naked woman running down the street carrying a skull, being chased by a crazed mercenary with a knife wearing a towel would certainly make an interesting spectacle for the morning walkers.

Charlie sat down beside Drake and looked at him.

"What does it do? I had a real urge to *touch* it."

Drake looked at her then with interest. He hadn't looked at her like that before, not even during sex.

"You did?"

"Well, I mean, I felt an energy coming from it, like it wanted me to pick it up. And my chain felt hot, *really* hot. I probably imagined it. I don't think the drink is out of my system yet."

Charlie then reached up and felt the thick belcher chain between her fingers, rolling it between the tips. It felt perfectly normal again. She had imagined it, surely. Chains don't burn up all by themselves.

Drake stared silently at the chain for several seconds.

"Whose chain is that?" He asked, finally.

"I bought it on an online auction site," She replied "It supposedly belonged to Sidney Taylor."

TWO

"This isn't about speaking to my Father, Drakey, this is much bigger than that. We can cheat death with this thing!"

Drake stared out of the window of the cheap hotel room, down at the filthy, empty pool below. Morocco was a tourist hotspot, certainly, but like all countries, there were areas to avoid. And this was one of them.

"If this thing works, I just thought we could speak to him, I mean, I owe him a lot." Drake replied, the memories of Shane causing the familiar feeling of deep loss. The only real father figure that he had ever had.

Frank sighed deeply.

"I miss him too, Drakey. But he wouldn't approve of our ways. The last thing we need is my old man interfering with the incredible things that we're going to achieve here. Do you remember when we desperately wanted to learn Dim-Mak?"

Drake smiled fondly at the memory. Dim-Mak. The touch of death. As young, naïve martial arts practitioners, they sincerely believed that they could learn moves that could kill a man stone dead by striking various pressure points in sequence. Frank had gotten his hands on some material by a man naming himself "Count Dante", and for a while, the two of them had obsessed over joining the "Black Dragon Fighting Society", until Shane had laughed their ideas down. They hadn't given up, dismissing the man as an old fool who was stuck in his ways, and it wasn't until many years later, after training with some bizarre and possibly mentally ill martial arts teachers, that they had realised that the mysterious, supernatural abilities claimed by some of these men was pure fantasy.

"Your dad was right about Dim-Mak, Frankie." Drake looked down at the Samurai ring on his right hand, the familiar emptiness filling his heart.

"That's not the point! This is not about Dim-Mak. He was the kind of man to knock things down and dismiss them as ridiculous without even trying, without experimenting! He never once tried to study Dim-Mak, and yet without even looking at the material we had gathered, he told us that we were deluded."

Drake looked over his shoulder at Frank.

"He spent a lifetime in the martial arts community. I'm sure he knew of these fucking fruitcakes teaching bullshit methods and knew that they were full of it. The material that you gathered was advertised in the back of superhero comics, Frank."

"You're not getting it. He didn't try Dim-Mak. He took the word of others that Dim-Mak was bullshit, when those others probably hadn't tried it either. He didn't believe in anything more than what was right in front of his face. He probably didn't even believe that fucking elephants existed until the first time that he went to a zoo."

Frank sat down on the bed and took a sip from his water bottle. Drake stared at the man. His brother. His lifelong companion. The only two people that Drake had ever truly cared about had been Frank Jackson and his father, Shane. Whilst his own father hadn't been a particularly bad man, he had been a loser and a very poor role model. After his mother had walked out on them both whilst little Ashton was barely walking, Michael Drake had turned to drink, mostly leaving his infant son to his own devices. That had been when Michael's older brother, Robert, had stepped in to assist with the childcare. Old Uncle Rob. Loud, brass, manipulative, perverted Uncle Rob. The children's entertainer. Pongo the fucking clown. How Pongo loved children.

Drake shuddered at the memory.

He's dead. He can't hurt you anymore.

"Your dad was a good guy," Muttered Drake, "You shouldn't talk about him like that."

Frank absently swatted a mosquito that had been feasting on his enormous forearm, then lifted his hand to stare at the tiny splat of crimson left behind.

"Yes, he was, Drakey. I'm just saying that he wasn't like us. He didn't ask questions, he was content with his lot. He wanted the two of us to grow up and run the martial arts school, teaching kids, handing out belts. That's not me, Drakey. And it certainly isn't you, either. He wasn't happy when we joined the Legion. He wasn't happy when we went travelling. He wanted us to stay living locally, living dull fucking lives. He was a good guy, but boring people often are."

"He wasn't happy because he knew we would run into trouble, Frankie. You're his son, and he was like a father to me. He *knew* we'd run into trouble, and he was right. He watched us for years, getting into scrapes at school, with the fighting, the drugs, the knives… He didn't want to see us behind bars in some shithole country, and that's exactly what happened. I'm just grateful that it happened *after* he had passed."

Frank laughed, a hearty, mirthless laugh. He jumped to his feet and took the two steps to join his friend at the grimy window.

"Are you okay, Drakey? You've become a real sombre bastard recently. I keep thinking you're going to start spouting poetry. Cheer the fuck up. You used to be funny. You used to be a crazy bastard. The old Ash would be attempting to jump into that pool from the window right now."

Drake smiled and laughed softly.

"Alright Frankie, you big dumb cunt," he replied, "Let's do this. Get the skull and get out of this stinking country. It probably won't work, and we've already wasted a good chunk of the funds chasing after it."

Frankie took a couple of gulps of his water bottle. Warm already.

"That's fine, we've got the Afghan gig lined up in a few weeks. Then we can top up the coffers a bit. Where do you fancy going next?"

"I was thinking Eastern Europe. Cheap beer and hookers. Maybe hole up for a few weeks, find an MMA club, train, maybe even do a local competition or two. If we can find one with a cash prize, even better. Then just spend some time relaxing, empty our balls, have some drinks."

Frank grinned, pulling off his Oakley shades and wiping the sweat from his brow with the red shemagh from around his neck.

"That sounds more like the Drakey I know! You looking forward to getting back to Kabul?"

"No."

"Me neither. But we need the cash, brother."

Drake stared down at the filthy pool water in silence, pondering the task ahead. His spider sense was tingling about this one, but once Frankie had his teeth into something, he was like a Pit Bull. There was no dissuading him from taking that skull. And Drake couldn't possibly let the big guy go alone. Especially not when he had this horrible feeling in his gut.

"I don't think he'll sell the skull, Frankie. Not to a couple of westerners. I've got a bad feeling about this one."

"Then we take it, Drakey. We discussed this," Frank said, more forcefully, "We book our flight tickets today, then we get on the plane as soon as we have the skull. We'll be gone before the authorities even know we were there. I'll let you decide where we fly to."

"See, you're talking about the authorities. You know this isn't going down smoothly. I don't want to end up behind bars again, Frank. Tihar prison was fucking grim."

"We are not going to jail again, Ash."

Frank grinned his infectious, don't-give-a-fuck grin, and slapped Drake on the back.

"Come on, Drakey boy," he said, "Let's go and book some plane tickets, then find some street food and a bar. Don't think about tomorrow, it isn't here yet. Tomorrow is another day. We may both be dead by then."

"Sounds good, brother. I could do with a drink."

Of course, the Shaman was not going to sell the skull. To westerners or otherwise. Folk regularly travelled from all over the globe to see him in his isolated home, and for a good price; the skull was his lifeblood, his bread and butter. His shamanic practice wasn't exactly a hot spot for tourists and holidaymakers; his reputation was spread in whispers through the dark circles of those that practiced the darkest arts, and those such people were the ones that would travel thousands of miles for a consultation with him. His appointments were always during the twilight hours, and the consultation was not cheap. This was not, he would explain, a parlour trick. He was not a medium, or a clairvoyant. He did not class himself a necromancer, and the power was not within his hands; the power came from the skull. The skull itself was centuries, perhaps thousands of years old. Nobody could say for sure where it was created, or by whom, but legend has it that it was stolen by a deeply superstitious Danish Viking raider after he had murdered its previous owner whilst pillaging a land now known as North America. The Dane, known as Thorgrimm Redbeard, had supposedly felt its power, and had proceeded to take it back home where he had carved numerous runic symbols into the surface. It is said that he subsequently become a powerful shaman in his own village back in Denmark, where folk would travel from all over Scandinavia to visit him, after word had spread that he had the ability to summon the dead. It is thought that Thorgrimm became increasingly isolated, eventually wandering away from his village and his family to live alone in a wooden hut deep in the forest. Powerful men sought him, powerful men who wished to speak once again with lost loved ones, and those who hoped to use those powers for darker purposes, but Thorgrimm remained hidden. It was said that the legendary King, Eirik Bloodaxe, sent a party who finally discovered Thorgrimm hiding in the snowy woods, and when Thorgrimm had refused to demonstrate his powers to the emissaries of the King, one bad-tempered warrior had hacked off the hermit's head in a rage.

This agent of King Eirik had taken the skull, according to the legend, and then instead of returning the artefact to his lord, he murdered his fellow warriors in their sleep at some stage in their journey, keeping the skull for himself. This man, know later as Egill the wanderer, left Scandinavia in fear of repercussions from the fiery King, living a harsh life in self-imposed exile, eventually travelling along the silk road to trade furs for a living. It was said that he had gathered a small band of outlaws, men in exile like himself, men wanted for various crimes, and together, they made a much larger profit than by the fur trade by murdering other traders on their way, stealing both their coins and their goods. Egill's reign of terror, however, was cut short when he was murdered by one of his own cutthroats, angered by the inequal shares of the bounty, always in Egill's favour. Egill's killer stole his money, his furs, and of course, the skull, taking over the mantle as leader of the crew. The story has it that the skull has travelled the globe, being passed from shaman to shaman, killer to killer, forever leaving a trail of blood in its wake. Every holder, when he initially takes the skull into his possession, is supposedly required to soak it in the blood of the previous owner in order to protect himself and appease the skull.

Frank and Drake had heard these whispers, these rumours, these stories, around the campfires in the far-flung places in the darkest corners of the globe, where their travels had taken them. They had heard the stories from a cell within Tihar jail in India, from cockroach infested hostels across Asia and South America, from the criminals and human waste whose paths they had crossed.

Their fascination with the occult had began with martial arts; the old stories of the mystical powers of the masters, legends of the men against who swords would not cut, men with superhuman powers. Dim-mak became an obsession, especially with Frank who never did quite let go, even after himself and Drake had personally proven many practitioners and self-proclaimed "experts" to be either frauds, or largely deluded. This path had led them onto the occult, their uncontrollable need to make themselves more than mere humans compelling them to travel the world, visiting so-called masters in Voodoo, Galdur and Seid, consulting with Necromancers, Shamans, Satanists and Warlocks. Many, if not most, were bogus tricksters, petty magicians carrying out conjuring tricks to swindle customers out of their money; however, some of them did have true power. Drake and Frank had been shown some amazing things; supernatural beasts that live in the darkest cracks of the world, unseen to the human eye, dark spirits manifested in forms that their mortal eyes could see, and glimpses of dark, terrifying parallel worlds that those who practice the dark arts occasionally disappear into forever, to be eaten by the frightening beings that dwell there. They had glimpsed the face of Satan, and of Odin. How both of these deities could exist in the same reality, Drake had asked, how was it possible? The female shamanic priest that had showed them these visions in a shack in a Brazilian ghetto, a strikingly beautiful woman whose age could have been twenty of fifty, had laughed at Drake's ignorance. She had told him to pay no heed to any religious books, written and re-written by man, and to believe only what his experiences told him, and what the Gods themselves chose to show him. When he had asked whether God existed, she had said that the Gods are a race of infinitely superior beings, and yet there are again those beings that look upon the Gods themselves as nothing more than single-celled organisms compared to their knowledge and power.

Drake and Frank were informed by the Shaman, a man named Naja Haje, during their primary consultation, that in order to use the Skull's abilities to bring the dead forward into the living world, the dead would require a vehicle, a shell. A person with a strong connection to the dead being summoned would be the best kind of host. The dead being could not normally take over the control of the host entirely, but rather use their body temporarily in small bursts. The stronger the connection, the higher the chance of success. The stronger the soul, the longer it could control the body. Naja suggested bringing along a personal item belonging to the deceased, which again would improve the chances of success.

They had met Naja in a public place initially, a café several miles from his practice. There, he explained the process, and gave them the address for their consultation. His address was not advertised, and the only people to know it were those that he met in person in a public place, where they would be required to make payment in full. After taking the cash, he explained that the money would be hidden, that there would be no money at the address, and that after their consultation, his practice would relocate. Nobody would know the address less for those that he gave it to in person.

But of course, a consultation was not what the two men sought. Nor did they wish to steal Naja's cash. There would be something much more valuable at the address than money. Something priceless, even. What monetary value could be placed on an item that could potentially cheat death? An item that could be the key to immortality?

But of course, Naja Haje wasn't selling the tool of his trade. Which suited Frank perfectly, because despite what Drake's intentions had been, and the lies that Frank had told him, his plan never had been to purchase the skull.

When a Shaman initially takes possession of the skull, he is required to cover it with human blood.

Naja, an impossibly thin, yet wiry muscular man who appeared in his fifties, was an odd-looking fellow. When they finally met at his isolated home, he was sitting on a low table, cross-legged in the full lotus position, with the skull to his front. He was completely hairless and painted from head to toe with strange symbols in blue paint. Drake recognised some of these symbols, and yet others were completely new to him. Naja's eyes were milky white, without pupils and yet he did not appear to be blind by the way that he followed the pair when they walked into the room. Drake noticed that Frank had been on edge that day, quiet, intense, almost like he was preparing himself for battle. Drake too, felt the twisting in his gut, the terrible feeling of dread that he often felt during the hours before a stressful event. All the years in combat zones, all the travels through the dangerous ghettos and towns and cities held by ruthless militias had developed in him a sixth sense of sorts.

The two men entered the shack silently, standing before the strange-looking old man. Before either of them could speak, Naja addressed them.

"I will not be using the energies for you today," He had said, "As you have visited me today for another purpose. You know why you are here, so please, complete your task." Drake glanced quizzically at Frank, who, to the contrary, appeared to understand completely.

Naja had smiled calmly when Frank had produced the knife. Even when the blade had been plunged deep into his jugular, the smile did not leave his lips, nor did he lift a hand to defend himself, or make any attempt at escape. It took three long seconds before the shock of the situation had registered in Drake's brain, and by the time he had jumped on Frank, pulling the knife arm away from the bleeding victim, it was too late. The smiling, elderly man slumped forwards, slowly, as though in slow motion, the gushing blood from his neck slowing down to a trickle.

Drake shouted angrily at Frank, slapping his face, shoving him, asking why the fuck he had killed an old man, a helpless old man, but Frank remained calm, grabbing Drake's wrists. He told him to quieten down, remain calm, not to alert anyone. He then coldly picked up the skull and proceeded to rub it against the neck wound of the old shaman, still pouring with crimson.

Cover it with human blood. I guess the skull leaves another body in its wake.

He then calmly instructed Drake to change his clothes, before burning all of their bloodied clothing in Naja's open fire and then walking outside to their rented scooters. They would travel to Marrakesh, fly to London and then onto Tallinn, for Drake's planned rest and recuperation before their next contract in Kabul.

Drake would not speak to Frank for the entirety of their journey, with Frank seemingly unmoved by his companion's silent treatment.

He would come around. He always did. Frank may not be the nicest guy in the world, but neither was Drake. And besides, they were brothers.

The pair had spent a considerable amount of time in combat zones and visited some of the most dangerous areas in the world. They had become accustomed to remaining alert, taking in their surroundings and monitoring people around them to read their body language. Yet, in the heat of the moment in a remote, peaceful location in Morocco, in a post-murder haste, they had been sloppy. They had failed to notice, as they fled the scene for the sanctuary of the airport and the escape that it promised, a tall, sickly thin figure standing just metres away from the home of Naje Haje, watching them intently as they rode away.

The skull was not mentioned again for several months. Frank had decided to wait for Drake's anger of the murder of the Shaman to cool down, deciding that any mention of the skull might simply be picking at a scab that had not yet healed. Perhaps better to wait for the scab to fall off. Yes, it would leave a scar, but would no longer bleed.

Their time in Estonia had been good; Drake had relaxed, spent some good quality time in a Brazilian Jiu Jitsu school rolling with the local fighters, then some even better time in the evenings drinking in the local bars with the guys afterwards. The local BJJ boys had showed them the best bars, introduced them to some local girls and even pointed them in the right direction to get a few lines of coke. Of course, Frank knew that sucking Class A up their noses had a detrimental effect on the bodies that they had worked so hard to harden, but the few weeks before a work contract was always spent indulging in extreme hedonism; alcohol, whatever drugs they could lay their hands on (excluding what they dubbed "dirty" drugs, such as heroin, crack, crystal meth. They generally stuck with cocaine, weed and mushrooms) and sex. Of course, they would train hard too, always working hard, playing hard. Preventing skill fade with their combat training was always high on the list of priorities. Without their hand to hand skills, they wouldn't have made it safely out of a few of their more hair-raising scrapes.

Drake shot a man during their contract in Kabul, when their convoy of SUV's was attacked by a Taliban ambush during which one of their team took a bullet through the arm. It always amazed Frank how Drakey could so calmly shoot men dead time and time again and still sleep like a baby, and yet when Frank murders just one aged shaman, Drakey boy throws a tantrum. Drake had killed enough men in his time, and beaten men half to death in the ring or the cage; violence had always been a huge part of his persona; and yet deep within him, there was this pang of conscience that emerged occasionally like an annoying fucking worm sticking its head out from the soil.

Drake took pleasure in killing, Frank knew that. Being able to efficiently drop a man with a single, well-aimed shot in a professional manner gave Drake the same job satisfaction that an artist may feel when completing a sculpture and gazing upon his completed work for the first time. Just like he took the same pleasure in winning a cage fight with a swift knockout or submission within the first round. Drake loved to be professionally violent. Of course, he owed all his skills to Frank and his father. Drake had picked up a reputation as a fighter in the local area, at the young age of eight years old. He had been known to have beaten up kids several years older, and all the other boys at his school had come to fear him. Not Frank. Frank's father ran the local martial arts academy, *Bushido,* teaching various fighting techniques including Jiu Jitsu, Karate, Kickboxing and Judo. It would later become an MMA academy, but at that time, it mostly taught traditional Asian arts. Frank had been taught to fight in varying styles from as soon as he was able to walk, spending all his evenings and weekends at the academy, either training or observing, soaking up like a sponge every technique, every kick, throw or hold. He had heard of Drake's reputation, and with Frank's training, not to mention his unusually large size, he decided to show this Ashton kid what real fighting was. He approached him one day in the school playground and beat the shit out of him. The kid was angry and aggressive, and his fists were fast, but he had no real skill. The young Frank handled the angry little Ashton with ease. The school called both of their fathers; And Frank's father, Shane, couldn't apologise enough. He slapped Frank around the back of the head in front of the headmaster and Ashton, then spoke to Drake's father, Michael, at length. The man smelled of alcohol, and repeatedly informed Shane that he was struggling to cope with little Ashton; his wife had walked out on the pair of them seven years previously, and Ash was a real handful, always fighting, the school always calling.

Shane offered in a way of apology, to give Ashton free martial arts lessons. Full membership, all classes, to give the kid a little discipline and give him a channel for all that anger. Ashton's father Michael thanked Shane several times through his stammering, whisky soaked lips, clearly relieved at the thought of his handful of a son being taken off his hands for a few hours during the evenings and weekends.

More time alone with the bottle, hey, Michael? Frank beating up your son will probably turn out to be the best thing to have ever happened to him.

Both men then instructed the boys to shake hands, which they did quite happily. Drake was clearly excited about his free martial arts lessons, Frank content to be training with this angry kid that, despite his lack of skill, was to him, the most interesting person at his school. This kid had not been afraid of him despite the size difference, and despite being knocked down several times, he just kept getting back up to throw another punch. Frank liked that.

And there it began. Drake and Frank attended every class that time permitted, and also received one-to-one lessons, not only from Shane, but from the instructors in every discipline within the club. They both rose through the belt systems rapidly, passionately studying the arts and making Shane proud. Drake loved Shane, loved him more than he had ever loved his own waster of a father, and as he grew, he felt strongly indebted to the man. Shane had dedicated so much of his own time in teaching the boy everything that he knew, and asked for nothing in return. He didn't owe Drake anything, and yet treated him as a son. He gifted him his first Gi, allowed him to train for free, grade for free, and even paid for him to enter competitions. He would never accept a penny. Even when Drake received a little cash from his father or grandparents on his birthday, he would offer whatever he had received to Shane to pay towards training, but it was always refused. One year, on Ash's fourteenth birthday, he spent his birthday money on a silver ring bearing the image of the helmet of a Samurai, and gave it to Shane as a gift. Shane was visibly touched by the gesture, staring at the ring for several long seconds before speaking.

"You didn't have to do that, Ash."

"I wanted to, sensei."

Shane had laughed, and ruffled Ash's hair affectionately. "And don't call me sensei outside the Dojo, kid. Call me Shane. Thank you, Ash, this was really thoughtful of you." Years later, when Shane had been tragically killed by a drunk driver, the family had returned the samurai ring to Drake, a token with which to remember him. That ring, Drake had never removed from his finger again.

To Ashton, the training received from Shane and his instructors was the best gift that anyone could have given him, and although he hadn't realised it at the time, Shane had been a solid role model who had shaped his life and personality more than any other adult during his childhood.

Drake and Frank grew ever closer, becoming inseparable. If anyone messed with Ash, they'd also have to deal with Frank, and vice versa. They would spar together, go camping together, and talk for hours about how they were going to invent their own martial art style, just as Bruce Lee had done with Jeet-Kune-Do, but this style would include Dim-Mak, *the touch of death*. They were going to become the deadliest men on the planet, and some day, work as assassins.

They grew up together, chased girls together, drank their first beers together on a camping trip during which Frankie had vomited all over his jeans, and left school together. By sixteen, they were both at a high level of skill in various martial arts, and Shane had employed them both to teach a kid's Karate class. The pay wasn't fantastic, but by this time they were already getting to grips with Brazilian Jiu-Jitsu, holding blue belts, and fighting on the MMA circuit. But they wanted more adventure than their town, or even professional MMA could offer, and before they turned seventeen, had already decided to enlist in the French Foreign Legion. Shane was upset by this, wanting the boys to wait a few more years first, or at least join the British Army instead, but the pair of them had their minds set on it. They began to train, carrying weighted packs for miles, hitting the gym daily and even practicing survival skills in the forest. They would spend days and days in the woods, eating only whatever food they could forage or snare, and preparing their bodies for living with intense discomfort.

The training continued for just over a year, the boys earning their way by teaching the Karate class and assisting in the running of *Bushido,* then finally, when they had both turned eighteen, they packed their bags and left for Castelnaudary, "The Farm" to begin their basic Legionnaire training. And there, their travels began. They had never been cut out for small town Karate classes. They were to become the deadliest men in the world, after all.

Frank smiled fondly at the memories. Drake would move on from the murder. It hadn't been the first one, after all. Drakey himself had, on more than one occasion, stabbed his way out of a sticky situation. Four men in India had fallen to their blades after the group had chosen the wrong travellers to attempt to rob. Drakey hadn't mourned them, hadn't sulked, the situation hadn't even dampened his mood. But one elderly shaman? For fuck's sake, Drakey boy.

After the Kabul contract, they had decided to fly to Chile and spend some time travelling South America. Travelling, and of course, experimenting with the skull in remote locations. Due to the bloodshed that was known to follow the skull, the use of its powers was best practiced away from civilisation, lest they land themselves yet again in a brutal, filthy foreign prison. Frank had decided on an attempt to invite the dead to cross over into the land of the living, who the dead soul would be, he had yet to decide. Drake was keen on contacting Shane, his father, out of some sense of gratitude to the man who had given him so much, but Frank knew that Shane was the only man whose wisdom Drake would entertain listening to. Historically, whenever Frank had an idea that might seem to many to be foolish or reckless, as most of his ideas were, Drake would always be more than willing to accompany him, however, whenever the old man became aware of the crazy plans, he would tell the boys not to be so stupid, and Drake would invariably take his advice.

The last thing that Frank needed was for his father to speak to Drakey, tell him to get rid of the skull and steer clear of necromancy. Because the bastard would probably listen, and all the hard work would be undone, the old fool in Morocco would have died for nothing. No, as much as Frank had loved Shane, him speaking to Drakey at this stage of the game was out of the fucking question. So if not his father, then who? Neither of them had a strong enough connection to anyone else on the other side. The pair of them had sent enough people across to the other side over the years, but perhaps contacting a dead enemy wasn't such a great idea. Both of Drake's parents were still alive, as far as they knew. Frank's mother was still going strong, still running her accountancy firm, still complaining to Frank about his life choices, whenever he made the time to give the old girl a call.

Then who? When the decision had been made to acquire the skull, Frank had hoped that it would be a means to immortality. He had spent his entire life forging his body and developing his skills, his knowledge, always ensuring his superiority over others. His body was not a temple, it was a weapon, and Frank always made sure that it was sharpened and hardened regularly. He had studied and practiced in depth every martial art that he deemed useful, long after he had realised that a large chunk of the Asian arts treasured by his father were fairly redundant in a modern street fight or in the cages of MMA matches, he had switched to studying the more useful fighting styles such as Brazilian Jiu Jitsu, Muay Thai and wrestling. Always learning, always training, Frank also liked to lift weights, preferring lower repetitions of heavier weights, choosing explosive strength over the entirely cosmetic training methods of bodybuilders. Everything had to have a practical use, he wasn't in it to look good, but rather to create the perfect killing machine. All this work, he had thought, and so little time. His knowledge, his skillset, would all go to waste as his body aged and mortality took its terrible toll. His fanatical studies of the occult over the years had led himself and Drakey to some dark corners of the world and human psyche, chasing up noted practitioners and supposedly magical relics. Most of their pilgrimages in search of these people and artefacts had led them down some fruitless rabbit holes, however, there had been some strange and even terrifying moments. All in a desperate search of a means to continue life on this earth beyond the limits of the human body. As strong and healthy as Franks body was, it was, nevertheless, a decaying sack of meat and bone just like every other pathetic, whining waste of oxygen on the planet.

As long as me and Drakey boy stay loyal to each other, and as long as this skull is the real deal, there's no reason why the two of us can't go on for centuries.

Drake and himself had been in their late thirties by then. They had spent eight years in the Legion, leaving at twenty-six, much to the dismay of their Commanding Officer who knew that he was losing the two best *Sergents* in the unit. They had then gone travelling, seeking knowledge, seeking immortality, following a cycle of working in combat hot spots for varying Private Military Contractor companies for contracts of several months up to one year, saving enough money to head off travelling again. They would supplement their income on their travels by doing occasional work as bouncers or earning a little extra cash in prize fights, either cage fights or boxing. Their travels would normally begin with an investigation into a rumour, a whisper amongst the occult circles that they had come to know very well, where they would travel is search of someone who was said to have particular abilities, or to seek one relic or another that was believed to hold a certain power, then once their journey came to an end, whether it bore fruit or not, they would enter the next phase of their cycle, rest and recuperation. The word "Rest" was used rather loosely, as much of this period was spent training hard in an MMA gym, usually in some Eastern European or South American country, with the downtime spent drinking the local beer and fucking the local women, or hookers, whichever were easier to come by. Occasionally the two of them would pick up a couple of local girls who would become their regular fuck buddies for a few weeks, however, Frank was a little wary of this, out of fear that Drakey, the more sentimental one of the duo, might start becoming a little smitten and wanting to stay. Staying for longer was never an option; Work in some war-torn sandbox was always lined up to top up their funds, and to attempt to delay the start date would invariably mean losing the contract. Besides, the laying down of roots did nothing but slow men down. They had seen it throughout their years in the Legion, and amongst colleagues in the various Private Military Companies that they had been employed by. Hardened men, falling in love and marrying, then losing their edge. Frank had known an ex-Spetsnaz soldier, a cold, ruthless man from the wastes of Siberia, working the circuit in Africa. He had met a girl whilst back home in Russia, and from then onwards, spoke of nothing else. He carried her photograph and seemed to lose focus. The poor sap ended up being killed in a firefight following an ambush. Love, in Frank's opinion, was a weakness. Drake was slightly less hardened on matters of love as he; although Drake had never been in a serious relationship, and likely never would, he was often softened slightly whenever he met a girl that he "clicked" with. One such girl was a fellow contractor that he met in Baghdad, a female Latino ex-US Marine by the name of Valentina, a gym-obsessed hard case who for the first few weeks acted as though she couldn't stand the sight of Drake. Eventually, they entered into a "friends with benefits" arrangement, and Drake began to take a shine to her. They trained together in the makeshift gym they had access to, patrolled together, and fucked. Frank did like the girl, but he did worry about Drake entertaining ideas of bringing her along on their travels, or worse, eloping with her. And yet, to Frank's mild surprise, at the end of the contract, Drake walked away from her quite happily. They did exchange numbers and stayed in touch, but a romance it did not become. Valentina even joked on their last day together that seeing the back of Drake meant no more to her than scraping a piece of shit from her boot. Always such a lady.

In a seedy bar in Chile, sipping on cheap beers, Frank finally plucked up the courage to speak about the skull.

"Hey Drakey, we've had the skull for a while now," he said quietly, staring at the beer label on the bottle in his hand, "Don't you think we should try it out now?"

A momentary flash of anger crossed Drake's eyes as he looked up at his companion, as the memory of the dead man returned, his thin body slumped forwards as Frank smeared the skull with blood from his freshly pierced neck.

"I guess so. I wouldn't want to think that what you did was all for nothing."

Frank kept on gazing at his beer label, not wanting to make eye contact.

"You're still angry with me. You do know that for the skull to work, you do have to soak it in the blood of the previous owner? Otherwise, you never really own it. It only works in the presence of its owner, with the owner's consent. This was the only way."

Drake sighed and took in a mouthful of his beer.

"I know. Just no more, okay? I'm tired of the killing."

"Okay", he lied, "No more. I really think this skull is our ticket. All we need."

We can't avoid killing, Drakey boy. It comes with the territory. It's how we live.

Drake eyed Frank suspiciously, as though reading his thoughts. He knew that Frank would never have all he needed. He was a man who would always be searching for something more. The life ordinary was terminally dull to him; he would rather be dead than live a domesticated life.

"So," Frank spoke, stretching out his arms to the sides in a stretch, "We know how this works. Somebody has to be the host, preferably to a soul who had a close connection with one of the party. So, any ideas? Other than my father, of course."

This was where they drew a blank. This phase was, of course, an experiment. They would have to master the art of summoning the dead before using the energy of the skull for any useful purpose. Frank's master plan was that once the inevitable happened and one of the pair finally shuffled off of the mortal coil, the other would be on hand to summon the soul of their companion back, into the body of a host, willing or otherwise. Of course, it worked *better* when the host had a personal connection with the passed soul, but it was still *possible* to use any old body as a host, if the holder of the skull was practiced enough in using the energies. Or so the whispers said. They had first heard of the skull during their time imprisoned in India, from a thin, tall, wraithlike man who said that his name was Aayush, and claimed to have visited, with a companion, the shaman known as Naja Haje in a remote hut in Morocco three years previously and watched as his father returned from the grave through the body of his companion. He swore that his companion, who had never met his father, spoke in the old man's voice and adopted his expressions and mannerisms. His father, during the conversation, had told him where to find a stash of gold that he had stolen in a burglary many years before; when Aayush followed the dead man's instructions two days later, he said, the gold had been exactly where his "father" had told him. Aayush claimed that Naja Haje had sent his father back to the other side after their conversation with a chant that sounded to be a language that Aayush had never heard before. Naja refused to allow the old man's soul to remain in the host, stating that there would be a constant battle for control of the host body, and that if the soul of the dead one summoned was powerful enough, in time, it could take control entirely and banish the owner of the body to the other side prematurely. Therefore, Naja did not allow the soul to remain in the host for any longer than an hour. Aayush appeared to know much about the skull, almost as though he were advertising the prowess of Naja Haje, and both Frank and Drake listened intently to his stories.

Frank, on hearing the stories, had immediately realised that he must possess it. Cheating death was always the ultimate goal. Of all his numerous achievements, to live beyond the restrictions of his mortal shell of a body would be the jewel in the crown.

"How about we just see what happens? See who we summon?" Drake suggested finally. Frank poured the last dregs of the golden liquid from his bottle down his throat and stared down at the table, smacking his lips at the bitter sweet taste.

"Drakey, we never did establish how to get rid of it once it's in there, did we?"

Drake frowned and stared over at the barmaid, a plump woman in her forties, hurriedly and nervously wiping tables in the almost empty bar.

Oh come on woman, we're not that scary.

"No," he replied, still watching the waddling barmaid clean her tables, "this was your idea Frankie. I assumed you knew what you were doing."

"I know as much as you do, Ash. We both heard everything that Aayush said. Come on, you're the smart one. I'm just the good-looking one. What do we do?"

Drake turned to Frank, smiling wolfishly.

"You're right, Frank. I am the smart one. Which is why you, my friend, are going to be the host. You wanted this, you killed the old man, you got us this far, so you can now finish the job."

They packed for the journey as though they were packing for a military expedition. Only the necessities, prioritising the basics to save weight and space in their packs. Shelter, water and food, with very little else. Sleeping bags with waterproof covers, shelter sheets rather than bulky tents, with tent poles and hooked bungee ropes to erect them, and a couple of shovels in order to dig a shellscrape. They would carry a supply of water, but also a couple of lifesaver water purification bottles in case they needed to drink from the river. The food consisted of less perishable foods such as beef jerky, dried fruit and nuts, but the plan was to forage whatever edible vegetation that they could whilst in the forest, and snare animals where possible.

"Just like the old days, hey, Drakey?" Grinned Frank whilst carefully pressing his sleeping bag down into his heavy-duty rucksack.

Drake grunted in response.

They would trek deep into the Valdivian rainforest, overshadowed by the Villarrica volcano, and set up camp far away from civilisation and prying eyes. From there, they would begin the meditation necessary to attune themselves with the energies of the skull, and attempt to draw something, or someone, from the spirit world. Frank had convinced himself that no soul would be strong enough to eject his own soul from his body, and so confidently agreed to become the host in an attempt to learn, and eventually, hopefully, master the powers of the skull.

Drake wasn't *overtly* worried. He wasn't at all convinced that the skull was anything other than a prop for yet another sham artist of the type of which they had met several on their travels. He felt no great energy from the skull, and it looked no different from something that could be picked up from a thousand new-age stores all over the world. Frank clearly just desperately wanted to believe it, so badly that he would kill for it. But a couple of days in the forest would be okay. It was good to get out in the wilderness. Even if they were making attempts at conjuring tricks with a glorified crystal ball. Nothing to worry about.

Then why the fuck do I have this knot in the pit of my stomach?

No, Drake wasn't overtly worried. But the gripping clench in the pit of his stomach said otherwise. Inexplicably, he was more terrified than he had ever been in his life.

He looked down at his ring. Shane's ring.

"I need you with us tonight, Sensei." He whispered. The face of the Samurai stared back at him, silently. There would be no words of reply. Any wisdom or consciousness that had once been a part of Shane had been cruelly, swiftly and permanently snatched away by a drunk driver in an Audi, cutting away whatever years he may have had left, taking away any chance, however slim, he may have had of becoming a grandfather. There were so many things that Drake wished to say to him, regretted never having said to him. He would have liked to have told him that he was more of a father than his biological father ever had been, he should have expressly thanked him for everything he did. But Drake was never the type to say such things in words. And now, they would never be said. Sensei was gone. All that could be done now would be to express gratitude by doing all that he could to keep safe his only son, his legacy. Frank. Batshit crazy Frank. He loved the big guy to death, but he was as mad as a bucket of half-boiled frogs.

Still, they were brothers. They had always had each other's back, and they always would.

The trek into the forest was eerily silent. Frank, usually so talkative, said very little. It was almost as though they were entering enemy territory, the two of them unconsciously walking stealthily, scanning their surroundings for threats and using whatever cover the landscape offered to shield their approach from the direction in which they headed. The direction of the enemy.

The mood was melancholy, all joviality gone. Drake knew intuitively that Frank felt the same foreboding feeling that he did, but he also knew that there would be no turning back at this stage, no dissuading the big man. Frank had his teeth into the task. Once the dog had his bone, there was no taking it away from him.

They walked, sipped water and chewed beef jerky, occasionally glancing at their silva compasses or their GPS watches. Frank carried a map on which he had marked an area within the rainforest for a camp location, an area neither in ground too low that could be too damp, nor ground that was too high on which they could be silhouetted, and with a water supply close by in the form of a river. More importantly, it was an area that he believed due to the depth and distance from the beaten track, would be a secluded spot in which they would not be disturbed, leaving them free to practice their dark art.

The thick woods offered an occasional glimpse of the volcano in the distance, wherever there was offered a gap in the tall trees. Drake had expected more scenery, beautiful landscapes to cheer the mind and lift the mood, but all that he saw was trees, so tall that they blocked out the majority of the sunlight.

They walked for hours, never resting, always eating and drinking on the move. They would set up snares once camp was established, then forage for vegetation depending on how much their food supply had depleted. Hopefully, later in the evening there would be some fresh meat to roast.

They had entered the forest at first light, in order to cover as much ground as possible in the daylight hours. Frank had estimated that they should reach their location with enough daylight remaining to set up their snares and prop up their temporary shelter before darkness fell. Drake had checked the route and agreed, provided they continued without any long breaks, a task that he knew that they were both more than physically capable of providing no injuries were sustained on the route. Drake carried a basic medical kit, but if a serious incident occurred, there was very little chance of phone signal, and even less chance of an ambulance being able to approach through the dense vegetation. Air ambulances were a possibility, providing that they could find a clearing to use as a helicopter landing site in time before the casualty bled out. Frank always liked to have a medical plan, however, when Drake began to think about possibilities that were too in-depth, Frank would often dismiss them, stating that they were lucky, nothing bad was going to happen, and besides, they had been in much worse scrapes in the past and always walked away unscathed.

Frank had been right about the journey to the camp area. Nothing "bad" happened, and they arrived with enough daylight to administer themselves accordingly. Snares were set with wire with gloved hands, the shelter sheet erected. They decided between themselves that they had enough food remaining until morning, at which point they would check their snares and gather some plants for a good meal before the journey back. They had already seen some Chanar trees with their ripe, sweet fruit, and Carob trees, and they knew that they could probably find some Chilean Rhubarb and Strawberry Myrtle to give themselves some nutrition for the long walk ahead.

Finally, they seated themselves on their sleeping mats beneath their crude shelter, and sat silently, when the rain began to fall. The only sounds were the chattering and humming of the insect population, the sound of their own breathing, and the pattering of raindrops against the sheet above their heads. The raindrops drumming against the canvas above their heads further added to the grim atmosphere, lowering their dark moods even further. They were both quietly contemplating the act that they were about to attempt and the terrible, creeping fear that was slowly overcoming them, when darkness suddenly and swiftly fell, as though on cue.

Frank, being the owner, and the offering of host body, had the skull clenched within his large fist, clinging on to it tightly as his breathing accelerated into short, squeaking rasps. He knew what had to be done, but the terror was freezing him to the spot, rendering him useless.

Drake, sensing the terror of his companion, reached into the side pocket of his cargo trousers with a trembling hand, and produced a leather-bound hip flask. Without a word, he held the flask over to Frank and patted his tree-like arm with the lid twice.

Frank reached up with his free hand in the darkness, felt the flask, and took it.

Drake heard Frank exhale slowly as he unscrewed the little metal lid.

"Thanks, Ash." He whispered, before taking two deep draughts from within. Whisky. Good whisky. Single malt scotch. Good man.

He handed the small bottle back to Drake, who took a large mouthful, swirling it around his mouth, tasting it.

As though this is the last thing I'll taste.

He swallowed the scotch, smacked his lips, savouring the aftertaste.

"We don't have to do this, Frank." He said quietly.

"Yes, we do."

Frank's voice was a squeak. Drake had never seen the giant of a man frightened quite like this before. Not in any combat zone, not in any firefight, fist fight or knife fight.

"Okay, let's do this then."

"Yes. Get it done."

Before they had begun their trek, Frank had joked that using the skull would be like sex. The first time would be terrifying, they would be shit scared of getting it wrong and so worried that they wouldn't even enjoy it. But the second time would be sweet. And eventually, they would become masters at it. Drake had responded that if the skull's powers were anything like sex, Frank was never going to be a master.

That was the last time that they laughed together.

Will we laugh together again?

Frank sat cross-legged, holding the skull in his palm, resting his hand on his right knee.

Drake also sat cross-legged, facing Frank. He reached out with his left hand and placed it over the skull, over Frank's shaking hand. He squeezed it affectionately.

All the things I should have said to Shane, now will never be said.

"Frank, there's a couple of things I want to tell you.." He began.

"Ash, I know."

"This is important, Frankie."

"I know what you're going to say. There's no need. You can tell me on the walk back tomorrow. Tomorrow night we can have some beers, buddy."

The big man's voice was shaking like his hand had been.

"Okay, Frank."

They closed their eyes and began to breathe deeply, holding the skull between them. They weren't sure what they were doing, or even what they were supposed to be doing, but simply hoped for the best.

Just like sex for the first time.

The skull felt strangely warm. Not the type of warm that an object would get when held in a warm hand for too long, but more like a radiation slowly emanating from its centre, causing their hands to tingle uncomfortably.

They breathed. And breathed. And breathed. They were both fairly well practiced in meditation, an activity that Frank's father, the lover of all things Asian, had made them practice daily during their childhood. Drake had continued to meditate in adulthood, however he rarely saw Frank doing it these days.

Minutes passed, many minutes. Just breathing. Clearing their heads. They began to lose track of all time, as the tingling from the skull appeared to cease.

How long have we been here?

They breathed. And breathed. And breathed.

The tingling sensation had completely gone, and Drake noticed, he couldn't even feel the skull anymore, or Frank's hand.

Have we been doing this for an hour? Two hours?

They breathed. And breathed.

The sound of the indigenous wildlife and the rainfall seemed to mix into one, single buzzing sound. It appeared distant, like it was moving away, whilst Drake's own breath sounded to him loud, clear, slow and even.

This has been going on for at least a day, surely. This isn't working.

Drake breathed. And breathed.

Distant buzzing, slow breaths.

Where am I? How long have I been here?

He breathed.

Drake felt a swirling, sickening dizziness within his head, almost like he was spinning. Like a nightmare hangover, or like he was on a fairground ride, at a carnival. Like the fun fairs that Uncle Rob had taken him to.

I only had one gulp of whisky. And that was weeks ago.

Drake breathed.

The dizziness passed, replaced by a complete stillness. A stillness, and a silence. No longer could Drake hear the raindrops, the insects, Or Frank's breathing. He couldn't even hear his *own* breathing. Not only that, he couldn't feel anything. The skull was no longer in his hand. Nothing was in his hand.

Do I even have a hand?

He opened his eyes.

In front of him was a cake. A big, round cake frosted with a crude picture of He-man holding his sword overhead. A large candle, in the shape of the number 5, sat in the centre, piercing He-man's belly, with five smaller candles circling the centrepiece, the tiny flames flickering delicately.

He was sat, it appeared, on an oversized chair at the kitchen table of his father's grimy two-bedroomed flat. The kitchen sink at his right-hand side, as always, was overflowing with empty dishes, covered in dried food and surrounded by buzzing flies. Filthy plates and empty bottles of vodka were scattered on the kitchen counter. The room, like the rest of the flat, smelled of damp, of stale milk, and of course, alcohol.

Everything looked familiar, and yet, old. The old microwave, Drake was sure, his father had replaced years ago, it being the only appliance that the drunken bastard ever used. The television in the corner was a small portable black and white piece with a circular antenna at the top. That thing had stopped working when Drake was ten or eleven. And everything looked *huge*.

"Blow your candles out, Ashy." His father, speech slurring as always, stood towering over him, a stupid grin covering his prematurely aged face, wrinkled by years of pouring litre after litre of cheap vodka down his throat. Even years later, Drake could never stomach vodka, the smell always bringing a nauseous feeling to his stomach as it brought back visions of that disgusting, mouldy flat.

Standing behind his father in the doorway was another man. Tall and thin, yet with a large beer belly, seemingly out of place against the backdrop of bony shoulders and thin arms. He wore a multicoloured, striped comedy costume with oversized, round, pom-pom style buttons. On his head sat an enormous, green curly afro type wig, and his face was painted white, with a ridiculous big red grin over his lips and up his cheeks with a slightly uneven, poorly-drawn paint job.

Pongo.

Little Ash froze in terror. Uncle Robert was dead. He *couldn't* be here.

"Daddy has to go for a night shift in the factory, Ashy, but look who's here! Your friend Pongo the clown!"

Ash tried to speak, tell his father not to leave, tell him that Robert was a fucking pervert, but he was held in a deathly still, night-terror state, unable to make a sound less for a faint, slow, rasping exhalation.

Don't leave me here with that sick bastard!

He attempted to lift his arm to reach for the big kitchen knife that sat beside the birthday cake, but he couldn't move. His limbs failed him.

I'll cut the bastard's dick off. Never again will he put that thing near another kid.

Uncle Robert, Pongo, smiling, began to walk towards him. Ash looked to his left, looking for his father. He wasn't there.

He never fucking was.

Pongo walked around the table, never taking his eyes away from Ash, his smile fixed.

"Did you miss me, Ashy washy?" He asked, "I really missed *you*."

Ash tried to move, to cry out, but nothing worked. He was trapped in his own body. His own Five-year old, small, weak, frightened body.

"I've been watching you, Ashy. You grew into a big, strong boy. You worked so *so* hard to become big and strong so that nobody could ever…. *Play* with you again. I was so *proud* of you in your cute little soldier costume."

Pongo continued to approach, walking towards him down the side of the table that now seemed ridiculously long, metres and metres long like the banquet table of a Mediaeval King.

"I…" rasped Ash, finally managing to make the smallest of sounds through desperate, panicking lips.

His heart hammered, the terror building within him as the perverse clown drew ever nearer, the clown whose features were now beginning to look distorted, grotesque. His neck had grown longer, thinner. His arms longer, his hands bigger. His head appeared larger too, the grin wider.

"But you will never be bigger and stronger than me, Ashy. I'll always be big Uncle Pongo."

Pongo's body seemed to distort ever more, the closer he approached. Head and hands enlarging, body growing taller and thinner as though being stretched. His gait became more slumped, his back hunched, as though the weight of his growing head was pulling his unnaturally thin body down.

"You'll always be mine, little Ashton. Whether I be dead or alive, I will always find you."

"I'll fucking kill you!" Rasped Ash finally, snapping free from the paralysing trance that had held him prisoner.

He grabbed the knife with his stumpy little child's fingers, and clambered onto the table, stepping into the cake as he hurried towards his nemesis, squashing the "5" candle through He-man and leaving a small footprint in its centre.

The head was suddenly right before him, oversized yet strangely thin. It no longer had eyes, nor sockets, but merely two painted crosses in the space where his eyeballs should have been. His teeth were crooked, and tobacco stained. A terrible caricature of the man whom he had feared more than any other. The man that had destroyed his childhood. He smelt its foul breath, the sickening aroma he vividly remembered from childhood; Stale tobacco, like the smell of an ashtray, and rotting meat.

Ash paused, squeezing the knife handle tightly in his trembling grip. He held the point of the blade out in front of him, pointing it at the disturbing, smiling visage.

"You wouldn't hurt me, Ashy Washy. I made you what you are. Without me, you would never have become the man that you are today."

With a sudden jolt, like awakening from a dream in which he was falling, Drake was back in the forest. The sounds were back; the patter of the rain, the chattering of the insects. There was again darkness. He squinted, trying to focus on the shape of Frank before him, who appeared deathly still.

"Frankie?"

Drake noticed that he no longer had his hand over the skull. Instead, tightly held within his grip, was his lock knife, opened, pointing towards the silhouette of Frank. The Silhouette of Frank…

Is that Frank?

Frank's large frame would normally have been unmistakable, but he seemed thinner. His head seemed…bigger. His hair longer, curlier, bigger, like he was wearing a large afro wig.

Drake clutched the knife tighter.

It's not him, he's dead.

"Frank?" He repeated.

You're going to be the host, Frankie.

Drake's breath stopped, his shaking hand still pointing towards the shape before him. He could hear his own heart beating in his chest, rapid and heavy.

Then it began to whisper.

"It's not Frank. It's me, your dear old Uncle Pongo."

Drake kept the knife out in front of him, crawling backwards out of the shellscrape that he and Frankie had dug together. If he could just keep away from that fucking *thing* until Frank came back, all would be fine.

What if he isn't coming back? Pongo then becomes your new travelling companion?

"Stay away from me."

The lanky shape began to move towards him, the bizarre, unnatural movements seeming even more grotesque in silhouette as it crawled hurriedly on oversized hands.

"You're mine. You've always been mine." It rasped.

In a second, it was on him, pinning him to the ground. Through the darkness, Drake could make out the huge, grinning face, tongue lolling, as it laughed an inhuman, shrill sound that pierced his ears. A sound like a rabid hyena, merged with the pained laugh of a severely ill mental patient. A sound from hell.

"Frankie, wake up! Frankie! COME BACK!"

The huge face moved towards his, the long, lolling tongue dropping onto his cheek as it licked him. It felt cold and wet, like a dead fish.

Drake attempted to sweep the thing, throw it off, using skills he had learnt from the hours and hours in Jiu-Jitsu classes, but it was too strong. Unnaturally strong. *Unearthly.* He had imagined for years being able to bring this bastard back from the dead, just so that he could hurt him, kill him, let him feel how it was to be the weaker, vulnerable party, to be the *victim.* He had imagined cutting off the pervert's balls, watching him bleed to death, letting his face be the last image he sees before he burns in hell. And yet now he was here, and Drake was the victim all over again.

"FRANKIE!"

"I'm taking you back with me, Ashy. We can be playmates forever."

"Frank, I'm sorry."

He wasn't going to be the victim any longer.

The Knife came up in an arc, piercing the skull of Pongo with a disgusting wet pop. Drake twisted the blade, pulled it out, feeling the hot blood spill onto his hand, and he brought it up again, this time through the jugular. He went into a frenzy, ramming the blade in and out, in and out, and even when the thing had rolled off him, bleeding profusely from its new orifices, he mounted it, sticking the knife into its chest over and over.

Drake eventually paused, caught his breath. He breathed deeply, closed his eyes. It was dead. Pongo was gone.

When he opened his eyes, he saw, laying on the ground beneath him, the sightless, staring eyes of his blood-soaked brother.

Frank was dead.

He had killed Frank. His only companion.

"Oh Frankie, oh god, no…"

Beside him, laying in the wet mud, was the distinct, shiny shape of the skull, looking at him with its blind, empty eye sockets. It was spattered with Frank's fresh, sticky blood. *For the skull to work, you do have to soak it in the blood of the previous owner.*

And, unnoticed by Drake, from the trees, enveloped in the darkness, stood two tall, thin figures, watching silently.

THREE

Charlie sipped at her mug of black coffee in Drake's shared kitchen, staring at him with an expression that was part suspicion, part mirth. Was this guy for real? Surely, he was either playing some sort of joke, or he otherwise needed to be sectioned.

She looked from him, down to the crystal skull on the table. It didn't look like anything that she couldn't pick up cheap from eBay. Yes, she did develop an overwhelming urge to touch the thing earlier that morning, but that surely didn't mean that it was some kind of magical gateway to the land of the dead?

"That thing," She said, looking back up at Drake, "Can allow me to contact Sidney Taylor? Talk with him? You expect me to believe that?"

"No," he replied calmly, "I don't. But I'm asking you to come and see for yourself."

She looked down into the hot, black fluid within the mug in her hand. At least the guy made decent coffee. Real ground Java. Not the instant crap that she couldn't stomach.

"You expect me to go with you, in your car, to an old farmhouse in the middle of fucking nowhere. You, being a man who told me last night that he once murdered his best friend. You, who keeps two large knives close to hand in his room, and very little else. You, who clearly doesn't like me, and yet is capable of murdering someone that he loves more than any other. What fucking chance do *I* have?"

Every fibre of Charlie's being screamed at her to *leave*, to *get out of there*, throw the hot coffee in his face and *run*. He doesn't know where you *live*, and if he shows up at *Jack's* again, call the *police*. And yet, there was a chance. All the questions that she could ask Sid. Maybe there was something in this? Or maybe she just needed to believe. The story was far too fantastical, this guy just too weird.

Drake laughed, a genuine laugh. That had tickled him.

"Well the first impression that you had of me was serial killer."

Charlie didn't laugh. Or smile. She stared at him, waiting for him to give her a good reason, to convince her otherwise.

He looked at her, still smiling.

"I *am* a dangerous man," he said, "Probably the most dangerous man you have ever met. But I don't get my thrills from murdering young girls."

He placed down his own coffee mug, a huge, pint-sized thing, and stood up from his chair, opening a cupboard and peering inside. Charlie remained leaning against the wall beside the door. She did not plan on moving away from that door any time soon.

Drake pulled out a glass, walked to the tap and filled the glass with cold water. He turned again to Charlie.

"Water?"

She shook her head, eyes still upon him, eyebrows raised. He tipped back his head and gulped down half the glass.

"That fucking London fog," He said, "Left me with a mouth like Bin Laden's flip flop."

She didn't laugh at his joke; didn't smile.

He looked back at her and sighed, "Look, when Frankie…My friend Frankie… Told me about this skull, I didn't believe him, either."

"Frankie that you murdered? That Frankie, or a different Frankie."

He stared at her. Then smiled.

"The one I murdered. The same."

Still no smile.

"I didn't kill him, Charlie." He lied, "Not deliberately. We were in a car wreck. I felt responsible. I was the one driving, I was speeding. Of course I didn't murder him. I loved him."

Wow, Drakey Boy, you've become quite the snake. You almost put me to shame.

Frank's voice. Mocking.

Charlie stared again at the skull. A car wreck. That made more sense. What *didn't* make sense was, why was he so keen to assist her in contacting a long dead killer? She had visited a handful of mediums over the years, in the vain hope that Sid would come through and make contact. They all turned out to be bullshit. And what was the difference here?

The difference is, this one was built with arms like tree trunks, deadly, and wished to take her off to a quiet location.

Where nobody could hear her scream.

"Why can't we do it here, Ash? Why do we need to go to a secluded location?"

"Don't you want to visit the scene of the murders?"

"Oh, come on. You think I've never been there? I've just never been there with an obviously disturbed man that I just met drinking alone in a bar."

He ignored that one.

"It's five hours drive from here." He said, looking at his watch, "and the mix of the correct location, a piece of jewellery that he owned and the girl with an emotional connection, I think we'll be speaking to our man this very evening."

He rinsed out his coffee cup, and water glass, then stacked them by the sink to drain.

"Get your coat, Charlie old bean. We've got an appointment with Mr. Sidney Taylor."

Fuck it. Let's do this.

As Drake and Charlie had been drinking coffee, three hundred miles away in the portacabin office of a car wash in a small town named Thornham, an aged biker bartered with a hardened Albanian criminal over the trafficking of five Iranian girls. It hadn't been the first time that the old rider had purchased trafficked individuals. His car wash ran on slave labour, and these girls would not be the only hookers that he owned, either. He would set them up in rooms in one of the various houses that he owned, pump them full of heroin, and have his boys use a little violence to keep them in line. At first, at least. Once they became addicts, they were much easier to control. Threaten to stop their supply, and they would soon step in line. They would beg, even. Tell the whores that they needed to work harder to impress the clients, or their supply stops. Tell them that if they attempt to leave, not only do the authorities detain them for being illegal immigrants, but whilst in detention, their supply stops. Tell them that if they spoke too much, their supply would stop.

They were easy enough to bring into the country. Eduard, his agent and long-time accomplice, would promise them work in England. They had a nice job lined up in a perfume shop, a nail bar, or a bar. They would have their own flat, and good pay. Plenty of girls keen to flee from countries like Iraq, Iran and Syria. Eduard had even once supplied a couple of girls from his homeland of Albania. This was why John liked the old Albanian; pure psychopaths always made the best employees, and one-eyed Eddie certainly was that. Not only was he John's top trafficker, he was also very good at making people disappear. Young, old, male, female, it made no difference to Eddie. Eddie was not an employee of John McBride *exactly,* he was more of what you might call a freelance criminal, however, he had done more work for McBride over the years than most other clients, dating way back to John's days as a member of The Blackhearts Motorcycle Club. The Blackhearts had been home for McBride from his teens right up to his early forties; when McBride had finally felt that he had outgrown the club, he decided to walk away and go solo with his own enterprises. Sharing all his proceeds with the club, despite feeling that he was the biggest earner and hardest worker had taken its toll; he no longer wanted to fund the heavy drinking of those members not pulling their weight. The club, fearing the loss of a large source of their income, were less than willing to let McBride walk away, taking with him his personal prostitution ring, heroin business and underworld contacts. What they didn't realise was that McBride was the single most powerful member of the club, and that to cross him would be to kick a nest of very large, angry, deadly hornets.

John had his solid allies within the club, and to these few men, he offered employment. The rest of the MC were not quite so lucky. Along with Eduard, he took his closest allies and a few of his more dangerous underworld contacts, walked into the clubhouse during their weekly meet, and butchered every single member of the club in one fell swoop. All the club members were shot several times, less for the current President, Bobby Stark. Stark himself had a very different fate; he was to be used to set an example. Firstly, Eduard and three others tied Stark to his chair and restrained him, before McBride delivered his signature execution; with a blowtorch, he slowly burned the skin away from the face of the screaming man. Of course, his victims of this brutal method often went into shock early on, meaning that they weren't present there in their bodies, not *really*, and the suffering was minimalised as the unfortunate experienced an out-of-body experience. What this method was *really* useful for, however, was to ensure that others would hear of this cruelty. These others would be way too fearful of McBride's wrath to ever even entertain the notion of crossing him. Especially when the next phase of the plan was put into motion; McBride would send Eduard and his Albanian cronies to despatch the families of Stark and the other senior members of the club. McBride felt that he was acting in great compassion when he decided to spare the loved ones of the more junior bikers, although, he admitted to himself, it was more for financial reasons than conscience; Eduard's boys didn't charge a daily rate, it was a fee per hit, even when all their targets were within the same household. Fucking Albanians. Not even offering a group discount.

The message went out to all the other chapters of The Blackhearts nationwide; continue trading with McBride, do not seek vengeance. His contacts were far and wide, if anything should happen to him, instructions had been left for similar massacres to take place on every Blackheart clubhouse in existence. Therefore, it would be in their own interests to not only refrain from revenge, but to actively seek to protect him if the need arose. The Blackhearts were small time thugs, McBride knew that. He personally had raised his local chapter up from petty drug dealers and brawlers into the gun running pimps that they became, executing their enemies and even developing a network of police officers on their payroll. McBride had spread his personal reputation far and wide into the international criminal underworld. Without him, The Blackhearts were nothing. Keep him on their side and they may keep their fingers in the pie. Piss him off, and he would destroy them, and everyone and everything that they loved.

McBride was a wiry man of average height, now in his mid-sixties. Age had taken its toll on his appearance; his long hair and beard were pure white, and his face was a mass of wrinkles. Physically, however, he hadn't showed many signs of slowing down. He was still the violently aggressive, energetic man that had punched, slashed and burned his way to power throughout his twenties and thirties. His eyes were wide and wild, and he carried the air of a man who may, at any moment, decide to bite off your face, simply because he didn't like the way it looked.

Overtly, he was a businessman, an entrepreneur. He ran a security firm, three pubs, two car washes, four nail salons, a barber shop and a taxi company. They alone did turn over a steady profit, except for the pubs that were struggling slightly, however all these little businesses served other purposes much more useful to McBride. Firstly, they provided all his thugs, his employees, with genuine employment, on paper at least. A heavy whose sole purpose may be to forcefully collect debts on behalf of McBride, may have been on the payroll as working as a barman in one of the pubs within the empire, or perhaps a taxi driver. The man whose main purpose was to make people disappear may be "employed" as a security guard. Secondly, each little enterprise could each have other purposes beneath the respectable surface. A taxi could run guns or narcotics. With one taxi driver and a couple of "passengers" within a licenced, marked vehicle, nobody looks twice. Drugs and firearms could be purchased from the pubs if you knew how to ask; Cocaine was readily available from the barber. The security firm was a uniformed protection racket, the ever-growing company supplying bouncers for most noteworthy night spots across two counties. Of course, any club refusing to employ their services may soon find that their own hired security is soon unable to handle the growing amount of new and brutal "trouble" on the premises. And obviously, McBride's nail salons and car washes were all run on slave labour, the nail salons doubling as brothels in the more recent years during which John had decided to cut down on the seedy world of having his whores standing on street corners. That attracted too much trouble; the girls couldn't be watched closely enough, and it attracted too much attention from the old bill. Not all officers could be paid off; throughout the years, McBride had learnt that the phrase "everyone has a price", as overly quoted as it was on countless crime movies, was a ton of bullshit. Offer the wrong police officer a bribe for his or her silence and you could land yourself a heavier sentence.

Still, as successful as McBride's long criminal career had been, and as vast and prosperous as his empire was, and despite him being physically still a vicious, intimidating force, he knew that the mantle would need to be passed on some time in the very near future. He imagined retiring in a house on the coast, perhaps with a couple of his young whores to service him and keep his house and clothes clean, after liquidising a lot of his assets, including all the houses that he owned, and two of the pubs to give him some readies for leisure as he grew old disgracefully. He would leave behind the businesses in order that his network of criminality could continue in his absence; without leaving behind this generous inheritance to his loyal employees, he risked facing their wrath after leaving them without a means of income, and watching his back in his retirement was not the kind of life that McBride fancied; not when he could be relaxing, having his dick sucked whilst sipping cold Guinness and smoking cigars until his heart finally gave up. Whoever it was that would eventually inherit his throne was of no particular concern to him. He had children, true, but they were all estranged and as far as he was aware, not interested in taking on his criminal mantle. Eduard clearly had his single good eye on the throne, but McBride wasn't quite sure that he wanted a foreigner keeping his legacy alive.

The best course of action, he thought, was to let them decide amongst themselves. *Leave behind a power vacuum. Let the strongest rise to the top. Just as he had risen through the ranks - through the shedding of blood. Then, whoever was worthy of his throne would surely take it.*

John McBride smiled to himself as he imagined the screaming chaos that he would leave behind in his wake. The streets would run with blood.

The fact that Ash was clearing away all of his meagre belongings from his room and packing it all into heavy duty holdalls into the back of his 5-year-old Black Volkswagen Transporter van was again causing suspicion to grow in Charlie's mind.

"Ash," she asked, watching him throw the last bag into the back before closing the rear door, "Why are you acting like you're going on the run?"

"Because, Charlotte my dear, I'm going to bury you in the woods. I'm a serial killer, remember?"

He walked around to the driver's side and opened the door, then looked up at her.

"Finish your smoke before you get in. No smoking in the van."

She took a puff on her cigarette and raised her eyebrows.

"I'm not getting in that fucking rape van." She exhaled, deliberately sending a stream of blue smoke towards his face.

He turned his head to avoid breathing in the noxious fumes, the smell momentarily bringing to his mind an image of Uncle Robert, grinning through his stained, wonky teeth.

"Charlie, either get in or don't. I'm leaving."

With that, he climbed in and closed the door behind him.

Charlie rolled her eyes, flicking the half-smoked cigarette to the floor and grinding it out under her boot. She walked casually over to the passenger door and opened it, a sarcastic smile on her face.

"Why have you packed all of your bags?"

"Charlie, I move around all the time. If I'm driving five hours up the country, I do not plan on driving back here. There's nothing for me here."

"Then how the fuck am I getting home?"

"You're a big girl, Charlie. I can put you on a train."

Or a shallow grave.

"I don't trust you. You're a fucking fruitcake."

"True. And I wouldn't trust me either. Get in or shut the door."

Charlie sighed and looked down the street. A few youths loitered outside of an off-licence, hoods covering most of their faces. Across the street from the yobs there shambled a filthy, shaven-headed addict in a tracksuit covered in small burn holes and large stains.

What a lovely town. There's nothing here for me either.

"You know what, Ash?" She announced, jumping onto the passenger seat, "That shallow grave is suddenly looking inviting. Let's drop by my place to pick up some essentials, then let's get on the road, big man."

Ash smiled and switched on the ignition. This cocky bitch had started to grow on him.

Charlie's room was the polar opposite of Drake's. Clothes were scattered all over the floor and on the bed, the tops of the cabinets covered in various pieces of make-up, toiletries and empty rum and beer bottles. Arty posters adorned the walls, prints of paintings by Bosch, Paolo Girardi and other artists depicting sinister images, along with movie posters such as Stanley Kubrick's *The Shining* and a large image of Joaquim Phoenix in *Joker*. The room was filled with the strong, pungent smell of weed.

I hope she has some more of that.

Charlie pulled a large black suitcase from a wardrobe that was otherwise empty, zipped it open then began tossing all her clothing from the floor inside. Drake watched her, a questioning look in his eyes.

"What are you doing?"

"There's nothing for me here but a badly paid job pulling pints and pouring vodka," She replied as she swept all the make-up and toiletries from her bedside cabinet into the chaotic cluster of her suitcase with her forearm, "Maybe I'll spend some time living where he lived, drinking in the bars he drank in, walking the streets he walked. Maybe I'll meet a few locals that met him. It's something I've wanted to do for a while."

Drake continued to eye her with suspicion, a half-smile on his lips.

"As long as you don't think we're eloping together, what you do isn't my concern."

She paused, looking up at him through her flopping fringe with a look of disgust.

"Elope? Come on, Ash. I only even *fucked* you because I was wasted. Don't be expecting *that* to be happening again, matey."

"Did we fuck? I don't remember."

She turned away from his gaze, fighting a smile.

Prick.

"I'm going to wait in the van, have another look at the A to Z. You have five minutes."

"You don't have a sat nav?"

But he was gone, away down the stairs.

Prick.

FOUR

On any occasion that she travelled for an extended period in any type of vehicle as a passenger, Charlie would, after an hour or so, find her eyelids growing unbearably heavy. The act of sitting motionlessly, together with the vibrations and the hypnotic sight of the scenery passing by would invariably drag her into slumber, especially after drinking nigh on half a bottle of rum the previous evening, along with a quantity of Gin and Absinthe of an amount that she did not quite remember. Oh, and the bottles of Corona. How many Coronas had been consumed last night? She recalled polishing off four of them in her room whilst listening to Metallica before leaving for her shift.

Fuck, I need to cut down. Get back into the gym. If this nut job tries to strangle me now, I'll probably just let him. It would do me a favour.

"How many London fogs did I have?" She mumbled as she rested her head against the window.

Drake glanced at her. He considered for a moment answering her question, but before his lips could open, she was already snoring.

Lightweight.

He thought back, to his very first drink. Just himself and Frankie, fresh-faced teens sitting in the woods in front of a small campfire. They had acquired a huge roll of salami from the local supermarket, and had been cutting off pieces of the spicy meat with Frank's flick knife, then holding the floppy slices over the flames to watch them sizzle before snacking on them. Ash had managed, earlier in the day, to smuggle out a four pack of cans of Carling from his father's ample supply in the fridge, along with four bottles of Budweiser. The moronic drunk would have probably lost count of how many he had consumed in between his shots of vodka by the time that Ash had left the house with the beers, anyhow.

They had allowed the cans and bottles to remain cool by placing them in a carrier bag in the nearby stream as they savoured their salty red meal and the sky had begun to darken. They chatted excitedly as they ate, discussing the wild theories around the death of Bruce Lee; had he been murdered by other Chinese Kung-Fu masters for teaching Wing Chun to westerners? Or killed by the Tri-ads who had been the reason that he had fled Hong Kong many years before? They spoke of girls at school, and who they were going to fuck that year. Frank claimed to have fucked Joanne Stevens already; Ash called him a fucking liar.

He did fuck her a year later though. The girls always loved big, blonde Frankie.

Eventually, after thoroughly dehydrating themselves on their salami, they had cracked open a can each, then knocked them together.

The first of many, brother.

The beer tasted awful. Foamy, bitter and yeasty. They had both scowled at the taste, yet drank on, nevertheless.

They sipped, ate, talked, then eventually they laid beneath the stars, staring up into the clear, cloudless black sky. They had their whole lives yet to live, so many places to see, so many scrapes to get through together. They slept there, drunk and happy, content in each other's company, until Frankie awoke at around 3 am and shot a stream of projectile vomit from his mouth, covering the pair of them.

How many times since that moment they had looked back at it and laughed.

And I killed you, Frankie. I rammed a knife into you, over and over. I stuck the blade into your brain, cut your windpipe, pierced your heart. You were so scared that night, because deep down, you knew that was coming. You were afraid, trembling, over me.

Drake glanced sideways at the girl, snoring quietly. She had wrapped her own coat around her for comfort, and was now at peace, trusting the man sat beside her, excited at the thought of contacting a man that she had only read about in her true crime books.

I'm sorry kid. I'm sorry for the risk that I'm going to expose you to.

He thought of Frank. Frank's lifeless, staring eyes, looking up at him sorrowfully, the wounds, still heavily seeping with blood, covering his head, neck and chest.

That's just my body, Drakey. You're going to master the gifts that skull has to offer, then find a way to bring me back. We have many more places to see, many more beers to drink.

Drake looked again at Charlie. Cocky, sassy, sexy little Charlie. Just a pawn in this game. A game being played by bad men, for selfish reasons.

Get a grip, Ashton. This is for Frankie. And it isn't the worse thing you've done.

The room was dark, dark and bare. Rotting Wooden floorboards, wooden walls, no furniture less for a stained mattress that seemed very out of place in what appeared more to be the interior of a barn as opposed to a bedroom. What kind of a person would want to sleep in a place like this? Someone desperate. Someone with no place in the civilised world, someone feral.

She looked down towards her feet, and there he was, her quarry. Still gasping for breath, the fat bastard was holding his neck, trying in vain to hold together the wound that would soon take away his life. The wound that she had fathered.

She saw her right hand, bigger, thicker, hairier than she recalled, with mottled scars across the knuckles; her right hand, gripping a large hunting knife, wet with fresh blood.

She looked up, saw the girl standing there. No older than fourteen or fifteen, her frightened face plastered in make-up, more make-up than a girl her age should be wearing. And that skirt! There was something terribly wrong about her entire look.

"Susie, get out of here!" She called out to the girl, in a gruff, masculine voice that was not her own. A man's voice. "I told you not to watch this!"

The girl turned and ran without a word, out of the room, her frantic breaths loud in the empty space around them.

Charlie looked down at the dying man at her feet, considered finishing him off, a mercy blow, decided against it. Fuck him. Let the asshole suffer.

She tucked the knife into the sheaf on the back of her belt, then leaned over, grabbing the man's feet, clad in expensive looking black dress shoes, and began to drag him across the wooden floor, leaving a line of blood as his heart continued to push his life fluid out through his jugular. He was lighter than he looked, or, perhaps, she was stronger than she remembered.

She pulled him down the stone stairs, the stairway leading to the cellar, his head bouncing on each step with a dull thud as she pulled. She looked down at his round face for any signs of life as he slid awkwardly down to the dank cellar below, but there were none. He was gone.

Charlie gasped aloud, sitting bolt upright in the car seat.

What the fuck did I just dream?

"Nightmare?" Asked Drake, staring ahead into the traffic.

Charlie rubbed her eyes with the heels of her hand and yawned.

"Yeah, I dreamt that I was fucking *you* again. It was awful."

"That thought makes me shudder as well. Terrifying."

Charlie ignored his response and opened the window by two inches, sucking in the cool, fresh air.

"I need a smoke. And some water. Definitely need water." The dream still lingered on her mind, the realism of it startling.

"I have a case of water bottles in the back. But I was going to stop for a bite to eat. Are you hungry?"

They pulled into a service station three miles down the road where they stopped for a leg stretch and bought some burgers.

Not keeping that blade sharp there, Drakey boy. You haven't trained in a couple of weeks. You're drinking too much and you're eating junk.

Drake thought back to the strict diets that Shane had placed the boys on in the run up to a fight, or a tournament. They would both be weighed every other day, at first light of day, before breakfast, to constantly ensure that they remained at the higher end of their weight category. Shane would shed their body fat by restricting their carbohydrate levels, their only carb source during these periods being vegetables, all whilst maintaining muscle mass by vastly increasing their protein intake. Lean meats, eggs and nuts were all staples during the fight preparation. Frank would become so excited as a kid the day before a fight; Whilst Drake always felt the butterflies of apprehension, Frank never did fear stepping onto the mat, into the ring or the cage.

But he was afraid that night. That night in Chile. And that's where I buried him. Right there in the shellscrape that he had helped to dig, deep in the rainforest where he had been frightened. At the spot where he was murdered. He dug his own grave.

Charlie watched as Ash chewed his double cheeseburger slowly and silently. The vacant gaze had returned to his face, his eyes looking over her shoulder, staring at the large menu on the wall above the tills without actually seeing it, seeing instead something far away, something that he alone could see.

What are you thinking about, Ash? What is it that haunts you? What have you seen? What have you done?

"You don't look like the kind of guy that would normally eat this stuff." She said, breaking the silence, snapping Drake out of his trance. He glanced down at the half-eaten, greasy, salty burger in his hand, then looked up at her, with an almost guilty expression on his face.

"No, I mean, not often. Only when I'm on the road. Still, there's protein in there. You don't look like you eat this shit much, either. You clearly look after yourself."

Charlie looked down at her empty burger box. If only that were true.

"I do train in the gym. But junk food *is* a weakness."

"As is booze, and cigarettes. And weed."

She looked up, and strands of her long fringe fell across both of her big, green eyes.

She's so pretty.

"Weed? Why do you say that?"

"Huh?"

Get a grip, Drakey boy. Don't go getting all smitten on me.

"Never mind."

He crammed the remainder of his cheeseburger into his mouth, then pushing back his chair, he stood. Then, with a sideways tilt of his head, he beckoned her towards the direction of the exit. The two of them then walked back towards the van.

Drake waited on the driver's seat, re-tuning the radio in an attempt to find any station that wasn't playing contemporary chart music, as Charlie stood outside puffing on one last cigarette before their journey continued. The sun had begun to dip below the horizon, slowly sending the sky into twilight. By his estimate, they were around ninety minutes away from their destination, and the idea of again attempting to utilise the energies in that damned cursed skull had started to bring back that familiar, creeping feeling of dread deep in his bowels. He had attempted it on two more occasions since that first, fateful encounter with Pongo; The first time had been with a fellow contractor during a stint in Iraq on a protection team. They had sat alone in a tent and meditated, like before. Drake had made the decision not to actively seek Frank until he knew *exactly* what he was doing. This was not a botched attempt to summon Frank, no, this had been simple practice. The deep trance had happened just like the first time, except this time, dear Uncle Pongo was nowhere to be seen. Eventually, the contractor, a large Russian that they all called Drago due to his resemblance to Dolph Lundgren, had spoken in a foreign language that Drake believed that he recognised as German, a crying, pleading voice that started off particularly effete, then gradually deepened and darkened as the voice became angrier. Looking at Drago, he saw that his face had drastically transformed. Not simply his mannerisms, but what he wore was an entirely different face. Angry, twisted, sneering. Drake had shouted at the inhuman face, ordered it to leave, then snatched the skull from Drago's hand, tossing it aside. His colleague was then suddenly back in the room. Shaken, but back to himself. He had no recollection of speaking German, or even speaking at all. He said, when quizzed by Drake, that all that he recalled was, he had dreamt of being dragged towards the gallows through ancient-looking streets, with crowds of folk throwing projectiles at him in what had been a harrowing, vivid scene.

From that moment on, Drago had refused to go near the skull again, or to even be alone with Drake wherever it was avoidable. He had formerly served in the Russian Spetsnaz, and was not a weak man. Not a man easily shaken; and yet, a little touch from the skull, and he had nigh on pissed his pants.

The second time, Drake had paid a cheap, middle-aged hooker in Berlin to hold the skull, insisting that it was sexual role play. He had no doubt in his mind that this woman had received much stranger requests than this. The veteran prostitute did not mind in the slightest; sitting down, holding a lump of glass and breathing deeply for half an hour was easy money to her. Much better than having a filthy dick in her mouth. Or worse. Almost like a paid break.

Or so she thought. If only she knew the power of what she was holding.

The events that had occurred with the whore had been considerably more harrowing than the incident with Drago, at least from Drake's perspective. That evening was yet another that would haunt his nights, that *face,* that awful *face,* never quite leaving his mind. Especially all those nights alone, in cheap, dark rooms that followed. That girl was always there, staring from the dark corners of the room, watching him suffer yet another restless night. Her and Pongo, always there, with the faces of his dead, the men he had killed. The prostitute and he had sat together, cross-legged as before, the skull in the woman's hand with Drake's hand on top of hers. After several minutes of deep meditation, the hooker began to sing nursery rhymes, slowly, in the high-pitched voice of a young child.

Ring o ring o roses,
A pocket full of posies,
Atishoo,
Atishoo,
We all fall down.

Over and over she chanted the rhyme, in the sweet, shrill voice.

Ring o ring o roses,
A pocket full of posies,
Atishoo,
Atishoo,
We all fall down.

Drake watched, bemused, as her face became one of a child barely past the age of a toddler. The "child" gazed at him, smiling, as she sang. Her hair hung in yellow ringlets with a bright pink bow at either side of her head. Her eyes were pale blue, her complexion white and pasty. The face reminded Drake of one of the lifelike porcelain dolls that his grandmother had collected throughout her life, filling her house with the disturbing things with their glazed, watchful eyes.

The Grandmother that had raised Uncle Robert. What had happened in that bastard's childhood to cause him to grow into the monster that he became? That old woman raised an alcoholic and a child molester. Good work, Grandma.

Atishoo,

Atishoo,

We all fall dooooooooooooooooooown.

The song had stopped; the girl still staring. The smile was fixed, her pale eyes unblinking. "Do you like my singing?" She asked, a sweet voice, an innocent child's voice.

"Yes, of course.." He blurted, unsure on how to react, or how to close this one down. As cold and brutal as Drake had been in the past, he couldn't be anything but polite to this innocent young face.

That's not a child, Drakey boy.

The girl's face moved closer, still smiling, still staring, still unblinking. Drake felt a cold chill shoot up his spine, a nauseating feeling stirring in his stomach. This wasn't right. He had to put an end to this. Now.

"Stop." He ordered. "Stop there." A little firmer, but still polite.

The girl's head somehow continued to approach, whilst her body appeared to remain in position, static, unmoving, not even apparently breathing.

That's not a child, Drakey boy.

Almost without thinking, he snatched the skull away from her hand and rose quickly to his feet, staggering backwards, away from the approaching, unnatural face.

"Wake up!" This time, assertive. This was not a child.

The head continued to approach, the smile now growing wider, the eyes somehow growing larger, the face becoming a terrible, surreal caricature.

How do I stop this?

He let go of the skull, allowing it to drop to his feet, where it landed with a dull crack before rolling across the carpet and hitting the skirting board of the whore's chamber. The grotesque smiling face paused, looking down at the skull, then back up at Drake, who had backed himself up against the wall and was now reaching for his knife from his jeans pocket.

Are you going to kill another one, Drakey boy? Do you plan to stab the bad spirits out of every host?

He pulled out the knife slowly. Of course, he didn't want to stab a hooker in her own bedroom in a tacky Berlin red light district. That would mean serving a long stretch, if not a full life term, and therefore, Frank would be left rotting in his lonely grave deep in the Chilean rain forest, with no hope of ever being given a second chance at life.

The doll face remained in place, its eyes burning into Ash; he could actually *feel* a burn coming from those pale blue, glass-like orbs, as though they contained high powered lasers, or as though they projected the sun's rays being concentrated directly at his face through a magnifying glass.

"Do you want to see Hell, Ashton?" The child's voice asked, higher pitched now, "I can show you. A lot of your friends are there. They can't *wait* to see you again. A lot of your friends that say they are in hell *because of you.* There's a place there for you too, Ashton." She paused, as though waiting for a reply. Drake was ice cold, his body feeling as though it had dropped through an ice hole into the sub-zero waters below. His frozen breath hung in the air. He contemplated leaving the room, running away and leaving the unfortunate hooker to her fate with this… thing. He decided against it; he needed to learn whatever he could from these spirits, beings, demons or whatever they were. He needed to master that skull, he needed to know how to reject the *wrong* spirit. Practice would either make him a master or kill him in the process. But he wouldn't quit. He and Frank had each other's backs, and they always would. *More Majorum.*

"There *are* Gods, Ashton. Gods and beings that your mortal mind could never *apprehend*. Beings that, if you looked upon them with your simple, physical eyes, your little mind would be destroyed irreparably. Come with me, Ashton. Shed your mortal shell and indulge in experiences beyond any that these earthly confines can allow.

Come and join with your victims. Let them *embrace* you."

"Go back to where you came from. You're no longer welcome here." He said, as calmly as his shaken voice allowed.

The girl giggled.

"I'm just saying *hello*, Ashton. I'm not *staying*. I'm sending an *invitation*. There are many who welcome you. *Uncle Robert* welcomes you."

Drake held up his chin, refusing to allow the wave of fear that the name created within him to be externally apparent. He had already been through hell, right here on earth. Time and time again, by choice. There was no horror that he hadn't already witnessed, no terror that he had not experienced. No dead clown nor his ugly messengers were going to bring him to his knees. He was Ashton Drake. Legionnaire. Mercenary. Cage fighter.

"Okay," He said, with newfound bold confidence, walking towards the grinning face, "You've said hello, now you can leave. And you can tell Uncle Robert that he had better *dread* the day that I see him again. Because when I get to Hell, *the Devil him fucking self* will be shitting his pants."

He turned his back on the terrible vision, then bent over, snatching up the skull. He strolled casually over to the dressing table, pulled out his wallet and produced a wad of Euros. He dropped the cash. His brave defiance of the nightmarish creature that he shared the room with defied the mind-numbing fear within his heart. He controlled his breathing, remembering the hours and hours of meditation that Shane had practiced with the boys, instilling, in Ashton at least, a discipline of the mind that he had used to his advantage more times than he could remember during the darkest moments.

He stepped towards the door, still ignoring the doll-faced hooker at the other side of the room. Once he had reached the exit, he finally looked over his shoulder at the woman whose body he had selfishly used.

That's what she gets paid for.

The woman was back to herself, at least to a certain degree. Her face was again her own, albeit tear-stricken and terrified, black make up streaks were running down her cheeks, her eyes puffy and reddened. She glared at him, fearful. What she had experienced during the short time period in which her body had entertained something unearthly, Ash never did find out. He figured, she worked by choice in a profession where her body was misused for the purposes of another, for money. Still, looking at her frightened eyes, he felt a deep pang of guilt. She certainly hadn't signed up for whatever she had just experienced.

He let go of the door handle and walked back to the dressing table, again pulling out his wallet. He pulled out another wad of notes, placed it atop the first pile. He then hesitated momentarily, before pulling out the remainder of the cash from within and tossing it down, irritably.

He then walked back towards the exit without making eye contact with the woman, now sobbing pitifully.

"That should be enough for you to take a few days off." he said as he opened the door, keeping his back to her, "And I'm sorry."

"Just get *out!*"

And, carrying the cursed crystal relic that he had grown to despise, he did just that, heading down the street of the red-light district in search of a bar, and a stiff drink. Or ten.

What Drake did not see, standing in the doorway of a sex shop opposite from the seedy street that he hurriedly walked along, were two tall, thin figures, watching him intently.

Charlie, after her fatty meal of fried processed beef and cheese with a large black coffee, had become much more talkative. Maybe it was the caffeine, maybe it was her nerves. Or perhaps excitement at the thought of the possibility of communicating with the man who had been her crush and obsession since she had barely passed through puberty.

She chatted away, about great books that she had read, her favourite movies, her favourite bars. The more that she spoke, the more that Drake thought that this girl had led a very sheltered life. It seemed to him that her life had been spent walking drab streets, working menial jobs, self-destructing through drink, drugs and tobacco to a soundtrack of heavy rock music. A life sort of like a rock music video, and almost certain to be destined to be just as short.

Of course, he had the same tendencies of self-destruction, however, he had at least attempted to see the world and experience everything that it had to offer. He had often pushed himself into dangerous situations simply because that's when he felt most alive. The drugs, the alcohol, were always only used during certain periods, such as the final weeks before a deployment to a combat zone, during which he would not touch a drop of booze for the duration of the contract. On return, of course, there would be a celebration, but then that would be followed by a period of calm, where one or two beers would be acceptable, but drinking to the point of blackouts would simply not happen. Well, *recently*, he accepted that he had fallen off the wagon just a *little*. Training had slowed down, and the drinking of alcohol had increased. He mourned Frankie, he mourned Shane, and also, the faces of every man that he had ever killed kept flooding back into his consciousness. He saw them in his dreams, in the faces of people in the streets.

They are in hell because of you.

Charlie continued talking, asking him questions. What was his favourite movie? Favourite song? Fuck, if he *had* to make small talk, at least let it be a subject worthy of discussion.

"Why Sid Taylor?" He asked, out of the blue, cutting her off mid-sentence as she was asking him something about the best sex he'd ever had, "What's the big attraction?"

She fell silent, for longer than he expected. Maybe she was going to stay quiet.

I'm not that lucky.

"Well, he's good-looking. That was the first thing I noticed. But it's more the fact that he lived life his own way, away from society. He didn't like…. people. I can relate to that."

He slowed the car down, turning the wheel rapidly to the left, taking a sharp bend. Around thirty minutes away, he figured.

"So, what about the fact that he killed around twenty people?"

"What about it? I wasn't attracted to him *because* of that fact, more in *spite* of it."

"But that doesn't bother you? It is sort of a big deal."

"I think there's more to it than meets the eye, Ash. I don't think they were random murders."

Drake smiled, a mirthless, tight-lipped grin.

"So that makes it okay? Taking people's lives?"

"No, that's not what I said."

"Don't get me wrong, if you haven't noticed, I hate people too. Passionately. I think we are a species ripe for extinction. I think that the Gods are planning our extinction right now. I can't walk around shopping centres anymore; I'm afraid that I'll kill somebody. I mean, we are the only species who walk around bumping into each other. These people in shopping centres, I came to notice that they can't even see you, they can't even see each other. They don't notice another person's presence until that person is literally walking into them. Then they jump out of their skin, as though this other person has just fallen out of the sky.

Can you imagine seeing a herd of deer, or a pack of wolves, or any other animal walking around slowly in a field crashing into each other? You'd wonder how their species have survived. And yet, here we are, the apex predators of the planet, and that's where we are at now. People get so worked up arguing about how many fucking genders there are, and finding new ways to be offended, and the Gods are thinking that they finally need to wipe the slate clean and start again. I don't blame them, but for one man to think he has the right to walk this earth sticking knives into people and ending their lives, and then have people like you worshipping them as heroes, it's beyond belief."

Charlie frowned, listening to his tirade with a mixture of interest and annoyance. Everything that he was saying was really hitting the nail on the head with her, and she had felt the same her whole life about the brainless hordes that wandered crowded areas, but he was obviously personally attacking her regarding her interest in Sid. What was he, jealous?

"All bow down to Saint Ashton," She replied, "Saint Ashton the mercenary. The man who will take up arms against *anyone* for the right price."

"Correct. I'm a bad guy, Charlie. I don't claim to be good. I'm not interested in being good. If you had an irrational obsession with me like you do with Sid Taylor, I'd be saying the same. I'm not a good man, and neither was Sidney Taylor. Like me, he was a selfish, violent psychopath who cared nothing for the people around him. He used them for his own purposes, and if that meant cutting someone's throat, then that's just the way it had to be. And like me, he would have done the deed, then slept like a baby."

"You've killed people too, haven't you?"

"Yes, I have, and unlike these glossy movies and books that you love so much, there's nothing fucking glamorous about death. Each one of them is somebody's son, maybe someone's father. They piss themselves, some of them even literally shit themselves. When they know they're dying, they're afraid. They don't know where they're going, whether there is an afterlife, or simple oblivion. All they know is that they won't see their friends or loved ones again or see another day. Some cry like children, some call for their mother. The people that take the lives of others are scum, Charlie. I'm scum, Sid was scum. These people, these dead people who have had their lives cut short, they may have been scum too, but neither I nor Sid had the right to take away their existence. Yes, I've killed people, and no doubt I will again, but the thought of people looking at me, or at a serial killer like Taylor, like a fucking hero, makes me sick. Imagine having your throat cut by an asshole like me, or Taylor and knowing that someone out there thinks it's great. The only thing worse than me killing somebody is the moron that thinks I'm cool for doing it."

So that's what it is that haunts you, Ashton. That's what the glazed stare is all about.

Charlie fell silent for a few moments, gazing out of the window across the fields that surrounded the narrow country road that they travelled down. Dozens of sheep stood solemnly in the rain, chewing the grass, oblivious to the black van whose passengers were on their way to raise the dead. Sheep lived such meaningless lives. Standing in the cold, no shelter from the weather, eating nothing but grass, doing little else but eat. Perhaps that's what happened to bad people. Maybe they were reincarnated as sheep; wandering an enclosed field in the snow and hail, their wool coats soaked with rain, shivering and watching the human world pass them by. The lucky ones were slaughtered as lambs, the not so lucky grew to see their own children dragged away, frightened and bleating, to be used as meat.

Maybe one of those sheep is Hitler. Keep your eyes open for one with a little moustache.

Turning away from the sheep and looking forwards down the twisted road, Charlie noted that Ash was driving a little bit too fast considering the way that the route wound continuously down a dug-in embankment, making visibility impossible beyond ten metres at a time.

"There was a crooked man, and he drove a crooked mile." She sang absently, turning her attention back towards the sheep.

She contemplated Ash's words. He was correct, there was no denying that. There were women who wrote to convicted murderers, some that even eventually married them; Ted Bundy had masses of female fans; these strange women Charlie had always thought ridiculous. Sad, middle aged divorcees with a morbid fascination with equally sad perverts that had taken their sick fantasies one step too far and crossed the line. And yet, how was she any different to these people? She had a fixation on a killer whose motives had always been unclear; one criminologist had a theory that Taylor had been a closet homosexual whose sexual thrills could only be gained by penetrating men with a knife, the knife being a proxy for his penis. It was suggested that he had lured men there for sex and then brutally attacked them in pure frustration, sickened at himself, sickened at his victim, and yet needing that penetration.

Charlie didn't believe that. That theory carried no weight; not a single one of the victims had been known, or even suspected to be, a practicing homosexual. Some of them had even been married. Two of them were on the sexual offender's register for assaulting under-age girls, not a usual hobby for a homosexual man.

Charlie had always felt that there was much more to Sid's story. Those men died for a reason. Sidney Taylor was not a mindless thug, a knucklehead. He didn't simply stab people to death for kicks, not a chance.

"I am not attracted to serial killers," She said slowly, after several minutes of silence, "Sid Taylor is more than that. He's an enigma, a mystery that I want to solve.

Why did he kill those men? Not one of the victims were linked to him, nor were they linked to each other. Why were they there? How did they get there? The only vehicle that Sid was ever seen with around that time was a battered Triumph motorbike; nobody ever saw him with a passenger on the back. The men all drove to the barn in their own cars, the cars were dragged up later from a nearby lake. They went there of their own free will. Why?"

Drake chuckled quietly. This girl knew so little of human nature. A man could lure other men to an isolated property with ease, for so many varying reasons.

"I don't know, Charlie. Why are you accompanying me to that very same barn? Am I dragging you there?"

Touche.

"Maybe he was a drug dealer," He continued, "Or a rent boy. Maybe he told them he had a car for sale, a caravan, a fucking speedboat, who knows? Leading a horse to water has never been difficult."

"But why did he kill them?"

"Why does any serial killer do what he does? Nature, nurture, whatever. Because they're psychopaths, Charlie. They enjoy hurting and killing people."

"Are *you* a psychopath, Ash?"

"I don't know. When I joined the Legion, all I wanted to do was go to war, fight, kill people. I had no conscience, no remorse. I would say that the 20-year-old Ashton Drake was a psychopath. But now, I'm not that hot-headed little prick anymore. Like I said, there's no glamour in it."

The two of them fell silent, moments before passing the sign.

Thornham.

They had arrived in town.

FIVE

Thornham. Sid's killing ground. Sid's final resting place. Sid had met Nicola Donovan here, lived here with her. He had hidden himself in her flat when the nationwide manhunt began for a man fitting his description; she had protected him. Why had she protected him? Did she know that he was a multiple murderer? Did he lie to her? Did she even know why he needed to hide? Charlie found herself contemplating what she would do had she been in Nicola's shoes. Would she have harboured Britain's most wanted fugitive, a psychopathic killer that had moved in with her after leaving eighteen corpses rotting in the cellar of an abandoned barn?

Damn right I would have. If it had been Sidney Taylor.

The farmhouse, Sid's former home and Mausoleum, sat just outside town, a mile from the main A road that led on towards the city. Charlie had made the pilgrimage to the farmhouse once previously, with a clingy girl from school that had managed to latch onto Charlie and had taken to following her everywhere. She had been sixteen then, a few months away from leaving school. The two girls had brought some dark rum, Charlie's tipple of choice, some weed, a small CD player and their sleeping bags.

The farmhouse was quite easy to find using Charlie's knowledge of the Taylor case. She knew that it sat outside the northern border of Thornham, a mile west of the A road, the closest public building being a small Texaco garage that Sid had often visited to refuel his Triumph and buy food.

The girls had caught the train into Thornham, then from the town centre, caught a bus to a run-down industrial estate which had been the closest bus stop to their destination, then from there, they had continued their journey on foot. Charlie had insisted that they visit the Texaco garage, which had added some time to their journey. She had wished to walk around it, touch the fuel pumps that had felt the touch of Sid's hands, then walk around the interior of the building and imagine which foods Sid would have chosen, thinking of him standing there, paying for his fuel, his sandwiches, or whatever he ate. Would he have bought coffee there? Beers? Charlie thought of him standing there buying a sandwich, then tried to imagine him dragging a dead body towards the cellar, failing to match the two in her mind. It made her think, she could be standing in line behind someone purchasing a meal deal in a shop, a person who would later that evening be burying the corpse of a murder victim.

You just never know who or what people are behind closed doors. Every serial killer leads two lives.

After visiting the garage, the girls walked the remaining mile towards their final destination, the farmhouse.

Charlie immediately recognised the crime scene from the photographs in the countless books that she had pored over, the grey brick walls, the windows that were void of glass, the rotted wooden doors. Graffiti had been sprayed intermittently around the walls, random writings, nicknames, dates. One large, well-painted slogan had caught Charlie's eye; above the entrance to the barn were written the words "The House of Sid Skulkrusha. Beware, his soul resides within these walls", next to which was a door-sized painting of a skull head with staring eyes and wild hair.

Charlie's companion, Claire, had begun to whine incessantly almost as soon as the girls had stepped through the door into the broken shell of a house beyond. She complained that there were no windows, that the floorboards beneath their feet were rotting. She didn't like the stale smell, the spiders or the fact that the rotting door would not close. Charlie had reminded her that she didn't have to come along, and that if she wasn't happy then she should just fuck off. That had silenced Claire; in fact, she hadn't spoken again for an hour. She had tagged along as Charlie had been her only friend at school, and although she felt strongly that Charlie tolerated her rather than actually enjoyed her company, having someone to hang around with was more important to Claire than having an actual friend that she connected with. She had initially been attracted to Charlie as she had mistakenly seen Charlie as a kindred spirit, another lonely soul that needed companionship; what she hadn't realised at first was that Charlie was a loner by choice who tolerated Claire's presence merely out of pity.

The plan in Charlie's mind for that evening had been to drink some rum, create a makeshift Ouija board, attempt to contact Sid, then crash there for the night. Claire had been too afraid to try the Ouija board, and gave up on drinking the rum after two small sips, leaving Charlie to drink alone to the point that she passed out, sprawled atop her sleeping bag with the half-drunk bottle still clutched within her grasp. Claire had not slept the entire night, huddled in the corner of the room with her own sleeping bag wrapped around her body, continuously scanning the room with her torch until the batteries died, after which she sat trembling, listening to the snoring of her strange companion and the creaking noises within the eerie building, until daylight.

Charlie's plans to make contact with Sidney Taylor over a decade previously had been ruined due to her poor choice of partner, a pathetic limpet who was terrified of her own shadow. This time, she thought, at least her companion didn't seem the type to scare very easily. But what was his motive? Any sane observer would believe that the odd, van driving drifter with the questionable career was taking her to the abandoned farm away from the civilised world for reasons other than the ones he had promised; however, Charlie didn't believe that. As much as Ash could be a bit of an asshole, she didn't think him to be a sexual deviant. But was there any truth in what he had told her about the skull? He claimed to have seen for himself on more than one occasion the capabilities of the skull, and that it had worked *every time* that he had used it.

The van drove through the town centre, passing bars, restaurants and takeaways. A handful of people walked the streets, couples walking out for dinner, drinkers walking from bar to bar. All of them living on the same streets in which Sid had lived and walked. Charlie wondered whether these people were aware of the notorious killer that had made their town his home, that had himself been brutally murdered right there. Did they know? Did they even care? It wasn't the type of matter that a town would be proud to be famous for. Were they ashamed of it?

As they left the town centre, Charlie directed Drake towards the industrial estate, then onto the A road beyond. For the final miles of the journey, the atmosphere had become tense, with Ash becoming visibly anxious, his muscles tensing, his teeth grinding. The tension in the van in turn rubbed off on Charlie, causing the mood to darken. She began to question again his motives, wondering how she would handle this bull of a man if he decided to take advantage of her. She had handled plenty of men in the past who had crossed the line with their hands wandering to the wrong areas; these men had received a swift knee strike to the balls, or, in her youth, a flick knife held to their throats with a firm warning; Ashton Drake was a different beast. She sensed that it would take much more than a four-inch blade to slow that man down.

Relax, Charlotte, he's not that type.

With Charlie's guidance, they finally arrived, the ominous silhouette of the building growing larger as the van drove through the gap in the surrounding dry-stone wall and slowly towards the front of the building. The headlights illuminated the walls, the graffiti, although faded, was still there, the wooden doors almost rotted away completely.

Drake killed the engine, the absence of the noise from the radio plunging them into silence.

Drake, still tense, turned his head to look at Charlie. His eyes were bloodshot.

"Charlie, you don't have to do this. We could leave, get a hotel in town, then talk tomorrow."

She looked at the large black shape before them. It almost felt like everything in her life since stealing that tatty old book had led directly to this moment. This was what she was meant to do, she knew that. Whatever her role may be, she had a deep sense that she was fated to be a part of something bigger than herself.

"I want to do this, Ash. We've come a long way."

He nodded.

"You need to know, whatever comes through will use your body as a host. It will speak through you, move through you. If Taylor comes through, you will, I guarantee, make a deep connection with him. Just remember what he is. And what he's done. The experience may not be a pleasant one."

She nodded. Swallowed. Blinked.

They both exited the vehicle, and Drake retrieved the skull from a holdall in the back. The two of them then walked together in silence towards the door.

Drake switched on his torch and scanned the interior. There were signs there that people had used the building, empty beer cans, discarded chocolate wrappers, the butts of joints. The smell of weed hung in the air; clearly this place had been used fairly recently by smokers that had nowhere else to party. Teenagers, perhaps, that couldn't light up a joint or bong at home in front of Mummy and Daddy. Charlie bent to pick up a clear, empty one-litre bottle. Captain Morgan's dark rum, showed the faded label. Her bottle, a decade old.

They walked around the ground floor, finding the entrance to the attic, still intact, less rotted than most of the other wood. Someone had written the words "Welcome to hell" on the door in thick red paint.

"Do you want to do this in the cellar?"

Charlie, now looking nervous, nodded.

They descended the stone stairs, noting the faded stains upon each step that may or may not have been aged blood stains.

The cellar was musky and damp, hanging with thick cobwebs. Drake shivered as he noticed the remains of the gravel that had been used to cover the victims, still sitting in piles, woodlice crawling in and out of the thick grey stones, content in their damp rocky palaces.

Drake selected a spot in the centre of the room, a patch with less gravel than other areas, and began to kick the stones aside with sweeping motions of his boot, creating a space. Once satisfied, he sat, then looked up at Charlie, who was staring down at the floor, a look of disgust upon her face.

"I can't see where I'm about to sit." She whispered.

Drake brought his torch down to the spot at her feet, directly in front of where he sat, cross-legged. The torch revealed several woodlice and millipedes, swarming around mindlessly, reminding him of the masses of consumers in shopping centres, blind and mindless.

Charlie brought her boot down on the creatures, repeatedly, crushing the unfortunate bugs that had been happily crawling this cellar for generations. She had clearly decided that Millipedes crawling into her ass crack would not be acceptable that night.

After her little massacre had cleared a space for her to sit, she replicated Ash's position, sitting with her legs crossed directly in front of him, face to face. In his right hand sat the skull.

"Open your hand" He instructed.

Doing as she was told, he then placed the skull into her palm and told her to grip it. She squeezed it tightly, then felt his hand envelop hers.

"Have you meditated before?" He asked, in a whisper.

"A little. I struggle to clear my mind."

"As does everyone. At first. Just concentrate on your breathing. Breathe deeply, in through the nose, out through the mouth. Count the breaths to ten, then start again. Just keep doing that. If you get scared, let go of the skull. If anything happens to me, and something is in here with us that you're not happy about, order it to leave. Tell it that it isn't welcome."

"Does that work?"

"Sometimes. I think. But it all depends on how strong it is."

He produced his pocket knife, laying it on the ground between them.

"There's my knife. If you have to use it on me, then use it."

Charlie felt icy sensations in her spine, fluttering in the pit of her stomach. She suddenly needed to pee. She had never felt fear like this, and yet she didn't want to stop. She *couldn't* stop.

"Do you still want to do this?" Drake asked.

"Yes."

Well, I gave her the choice.

"Okay, let's begin."

They breathed deeply. In and out, in and out. To Charlie, it sounded as though their inhalations and exhalations were perfectly in sync. They breathed, and she attempted to clear her mind.

Count the breaths.

One, two…

Freddy's coming for you.

One, two…

I can't clear my fucking head.

One, two, three…

I'm scared.

One, two, three, four…

What does he mean, if something happens to him? What's going to happen? I don't want to be alone with something… something terrible…

One, two…

I haven't even counted to five yet.

Three…

If something happens to him, where the fuck are his van keys?

Four…

This skull feels hot. Am I imagining that?

One, two, three, four, five…

I made it to five..

One, two, three, four, five, six, seven..

The skull's temperature appeared to be rising and rising, as again did the silver chain around her neck. The skull had called to her that morning, *wanting* her to do this. This had been her purpose all along. She was meant for something, she was a pawn in all of this. Maybe more than that, perhaps even a *Queen.*

Then, she was outside of the barn, and it was early evening, the sun only just beginning to sink into the horizon. The graffiti had gone, the front door intact. She approached the door, paused. Glancing to her left, she saw, parked at the side of the building, a shiny Harley Davidson motorcycle. A visitor.

Charlie reached down to her boot and pulled out the knife that she had concealed within, stepped back from the door, then, after a brief pause, kicked the door in hard and ran inside.

After two bounds, she paused. Paused and stared at the bundle on the floor, a bloody, lifeless bundle.

Susie.

"Don't move a fucking muscle." The voice was deep, gruff, angry. Her eyes glanced to the right, looking straight down the barrel of a black handgun, aimed straight at her temple.

"She's fucking dead," Said the voice, "Don't worry about that little cunt. You'll be joining her soon enough, Taylor. Did you really think you could fuck with John McBride? Get on your knees."

She did as she was told. She knelt, placed her hands on her head, staring down at the corpse of the girl, the anger rising within her.

"Here's what's going to happen. Steve will be here soon with the van. We will be taking you to Mr. McBride. When he hears of this, I'm sure he'll want to set an example. You're nobody, Taylor, you're nothing. You and this little whore thinking that you could pull the wool over our eyes, it's fucking laughable. You'll be joining your bodies in the cellar really soon, if you're fucking lucky."

Charlie moved fast. She grabbed his wrist, pushing the gun hand away from line of sight of her head whilst simultaneously jumping to her feet. A shot rang out, a split second before she delivered a powerful head-butt to the gunman's nose. He was clearly a biker, long haired, long bearded, wearing a leather sleeveless jacket with a badge that bore the words "Blackhearts MC", above another that read "Thornham Chapter".

The blow knocked him backwards, dropping him onto his back, whilst Charlie kept hold of the wrist, keeping the pistol pointing up towards the ceiling. She then stepped onto his throat, pulling his arm with both hands, causing him to croak loudly.

"Let go of the fucking gun." She growled in a masculine voice.

Charlie wrenched the weapon from his grip before dropping his arm and stepping away. She looked down again at the unfortunate girl, before spinning suddenly and delivering a hard kick to the belly of the biker, followed by another, then another. He retched, doubling over in pain as he curled into a foetal position on the bloody ground.

"She was fourteen years old," She snarled angrily, "fourteen! And you were pimping her out. You were pimping a fucking child!"

Another kick.

"Pimping her out, and then you fucking kill her."

Charlie squatted before the man, who was trying to regulate his breathing. She brought her face close to his, brushing back a strand of hair that had fallen across her eye.

"I'm really going to take my time with you. You're going to suffer. If McBride wants an example, then I'll give him one. I look forward to Steve arriving."

She tucked the pistol into the back of her jeans, then raised her boot knife up, the blade pointing towards the bikers' eye.

Drake had sunk into a deep meditative trance, almost unconscious, when he heard the breathing. Not his own deep, slow breaths, nor the breathing of Charlie that had somehow fallen in line with his own, but a rasping series of short breaths. And not the sound of a single person, but several of them, scattered around the room.

His eyes snapped open, and he blinked, squinted, attempting to adjust his vision to the darkness around him. He saw Charlie before him, her shoulders rising and falling with each breath, the skull still firmly clamped in her grip. He squinted again, staring beyond, at the hoarse sounds in the room behind her. Drake fumbled for his torch, felt it, clicked the switch. Nothing. It was dead. He leaned his head forwards, and as his eyes adjusted to the gloom, he began to be able to make out the shapes of figures standing around them, in a circle around the room. They didn't speak, didn't approach, merely watched, silent apart from the sounds of the croaky inhalations and exhalations.

Ignore them, Drakey boy. Just focus. They're just the folk from this room.

Drake closed his eyes, feeling the cold shivers that always accompanied the presence of the dead, the ice in the spine. Of course he was afraid, and he did not enjoy having the dead standing behind him in this dark, dank cellar, however, the show must go on. He focused again on his own breathing, focusing his mind, always keeping up the self-discipline that Shane had taught him.

He took a few deep breaths, then opened his eyes again, looked at Charlie.

But it wasn't Charlie. The build was larger, the hair different. A man.

Taylor?

"Ashton, it's me." A voice he recognised. A warm, comforting voice.

"Shane?"

"Yes, Ash. It's me. I don't have much time to talk, there are some here more powerful than myself. You need to stop this now."

"Shane, how? I haven't figured out how yet."

"He hasn't latched onto her yet. Take the skull from her, and he won't get a chance. Be quick."

"But, this is for Frank, Sensei. You know what I did to him, don't you?"

"Yes, I know. It wasn't your fault. Frank is fine. Don't worry about Frank. What you're trying to do with my son will just cause more pain for you, and for him. Just walk away, Ash. Smash that skull. You're putting this girl at risk. I know you have a conscience in there, somewhere. Don't do this to her."

"I owe it to Frank. It's what he wanted."

No response.

"Shane?"

Nothing. Drake squinted, stared at Charlie. Still a heavily-built man. But it wasn't Shane; this man was bigger than Shane. The breathing from the shapes in the darkness had intensified, quickened, become louder. Almost like they were panicking. Someone else was in the room with them. Someone that they were afraid of. The breathing appeared to stop, then suddenly, in unison, they began to moan pitifully, as though in pain.

Daddy's home. Fuck this.

Drake pulled at the skull, attempting to wrench it from the grasp of the figure before him, and failed. The grip was tight, like a vice. He pulled again. He had to stop this. This had all been a big mistake, what was he thinking?

The figures standing around the room had now begun to scream in terror, shrill, piercing cries that were hurting Drake's ears.

He pushed his foot out, towards Charlie (Or *Sidney?*) and pushed into the stomach area with his sole as he pulled at the arm holding the skull, twisting it around until it had gone one hundred and eighty degrees, then with his other hand, finally loosened the thing from the large, powerful hand.

The figure growled, a threatening sound like a tiger warning away a scavenger from its freshly hunted meal. Drake threw the skull aside, into the gravel. The screaming of the shapes calmed, dying down into a long sigh.

"Charlie! Wake up!"

Drake kept the grip on her wrist, twisting it uncomfortably into a painful wrist lock, her palm facing upwards. He couldn't afford to enter into a physical fight with whatever it was that had taken refuge in her body, he couldn't risk taking another life over that wretched skull. He *wouldn't*.

The shape didn't struggle, or fight. The figures in the room seemed to have disappeared back into the darkness, again at peace.

"Charlie?"

"You're hurting me." A calm, reasoned voice. No sound of fear, no wobble in the voice, no apparent tears.

"Is that you, Charlie?"

He released the tension on her wrist, not letting go, not yet, but easing the pain a little. The shape of the large man had gone; the smaller, thinner outline of the girl remained.

"Yes, it's me. Let go."

A moment's hesitation, then he released his grip.

"Let's get out of here."

Picking up the skull, they walked back up the stairs steadily, feeling the wall for guidance. Drake walked in front, with Charlie holding his shoulder. Drake felt good about that; almost as though she wanted his protection, although in reality, he knew that she was merely allowing him to lead her out of that revolting room.

They returned to the van quietly, not speaking until after climbing into their respective seats in the vehicle and closing the doors behind them. Then, there were a few seconds of mutual silence, both of them allowing the peculiar, disturbing events that had just occurred to sink into their minds. Finally, Charlie broke the silence, speaking calmly and clearly.

"I understand it all now. I saw some of what happened."

Drake turned his head to look at her, listening.

"Sid Taylor stayed here for a while. This place was also used by a child prostitute who was being pimped out by The Blackhearts. The fucking perverts that paid for her used to pick this girl Susie up and drive her here, out of the way. They would do whatever they wanted with her, give her the cash, then take her back. When Sid moved in, he saw this girl show up one day with a man. When this man started… you know…Well, Sid killed this guy, thinking he was witnessing a child being raped. Susie was terrified, no doubt. But somehow, they made an alliance. Sid's plan was, Susie would bring the men back there to the farm, Sid would kill them, then the two of them would split whatever cash these sick bastards had in their wallets. Susie could then pay whatever she needed to pay to The Blackhearts, and have some money left over. Sid would drive her close to town in the dead man's car, then drive the car to the lake to ditch it, as soon as darkness fell."

Drake listened quietly.

"Then one day, somehow, The Blackhearts figured it out," She continued, becoming slightly more excited, clearly elated that her enigma had finally been solved, "They must have noticed that regulars were no longer coming back and became suspicious. One biker who had been Susie's handler decided to take her to the farm to have a look around. She was very reluctant, and clearly afraid to go back there, knowing that this biker was going to find the bodies, which he did. He arranged for another member of the gang to collect a van and follow on to the farm. He already suspected that Sid Taylor may be involved, as Sid was known to The Blackhearts and had been for many years. They knew that he had been seen around the area of the farm, but never did they believe that even he would have had the balls to interfere with their business.

When the bodies were found, Susie was beaten, then shot dead by this prick. Then Sid showed up. He tortured this guy to death in retaliation for killing the girl, then when his friend showed up with the van, Sid beat him to death.

These two men were not left in the cellar with the others, these were not known victims. Other members of The Blackhearts must have visited the farm later to chase these two up after they didn't return. They probably buried their own and left the other bodies in the cellar. They didn't go to the police, as that's not how they operated.

Sid didn't go back to the farm, he moved on, but not far. He must not have realised the danger, not knowing that other Blackhearts suspected him. He rented a room in town and shortly afterwards moved in with Nicola Donovan.

I don't know about much of what happened after this, he didn't show me. But I do know that he was killed by a man named John McBride."

"John *McBride*?" Drake laughed, "What a fucking surprise."

Whenever Drake and Frank had returned from a contract, more often than not they would return to the UK for a few weeks, in what they called the Re-org. They would find somewhere to stay, plan their next movements, book flights, arrange a new contract for a few months down the line. During these short periods, using their security contracts, they would find temporary work such as short-term Close Protection jobs, event security and door work. One company, Valhalla Security, provided door staff for several nightclubs in the northern counties. Frank and Drake had built up a good relationship with the director of the company, a man named Will Bromley. He had often provided them work whenever they were back on home soil, or at least pointed them towards other companies that required temporary staff. On one particular occasion, they had visited him in his office to find him looking dishevelled and red eyed. He was apologetic, informing them that he had no work to offer them; that he was struggling to even keep his permanent staff employed. Drake and Frank had taken seats in his office, Drake offering the man his hip flask. They had a drink together, and Bromley had told the two of them that he had been bullied out of most of the clubs that he had previously provided security for. A man named John McBride, whose security company was little more than a protection racket with a website, had taken over all the notable clubs across three counties. Club owners with whom Bromley had previously had a good working relationship had turned cold; they offered little explanation other than that they were now using McBride's security, the contract between them would be terminated with immediate effect.

From there, Drake and Frank had struggled to nail down any employment in door or event work in the areas in which they were familiar, and with the companies that knew them, causing them to travel a considerable distance south before they could escape the all-encompassing net that McBride seemed to have over the security industry. They had been in touch with McBride's company, imaginatively named McBride Security, but despite their impressive portfolio of security work, McBride Security were far from interested.

Drake had conducted his own investigation into the man, discovering that he was a kingpin in drugs and firearms, and that he employed only those in the criminal underworld that showed him a degree of loyalty. For instance, a bouncer working for McBride would very likely be dealing in narcotics in the very club that he was employed to protect, and perhaps also doing enforcement for McBride's interests on the side. Outsiders not known to his extended network would not be welcome. Frank and Drake had always had their own criminal contacts, occasionally carrying out well-paid tasks, tasks that required men with tactical skillset, men who were not known criminals. They had, in the past, kidnapped a banker, delivered a vicious beating to a drug dealer who was selling dirty heroin in the wrong area, and on one occasion that Drake was not proud of, they killed a man who had supposedly raped the wife of a high-level gangland boss. Drake preferred not to become to close to these particular contacts, and liked to pick and choose the jobs that they offered, but they were nevertheless a good source of fast income. Drake spoke to these contacts about McBride, all of whom warned the two of them to stay away from him. He was a feared man.

"You know John McBride?" Charlie asked, "You really are a shady bastard, Ash."

"Not like that, he's no friend of mine. All I know is that he's the head of a criminal network based in this part of the country. He has legitimate businesses as a front for his activities, all over the place. People are afraid of him."

"Are *you* afraid of him?"

Drake laughed.

"No. But I have no quarrel with him, so why should I be? You have no quarrel with him, either, Charlie. Whatever happened between him and Taylor was between him and Taylor. Let's just get some sleep, and in the morning, I'll take you wherever you want to go. I have blankets in the back, you can get some rest back there. I'll sleep here in the front."

"You have no quarrel with a man who pimps out children?"

Drake turned to her. Was she really that deluded? What did she think he was, some sort of vigilante? A one-man army?

"Who do you think I am, Charlie? The Punisher? McBride isn't my problem. Get some sleep."

Charlie shrugged, resigned. Maybe he was right. The two of them couldn't exactly bring down a large criminal network by themselves, driving around in a van, armed with Ash's little knife. Sid, Nicola and little Susie would have to go unavenged. Like Ash had said, it wasn't their fight. If the police couldn't bring down McBride, what did a drunken barmaid expect to do with her PTSD stricken sidekick?

Ash's dreams were troubled, as always. He saw, like every other night, the faces that haunted him. Frank, his glassy eyes staring accusingly, the twisted face of Pongo the clown, the doll-like child's face of the possessed prostitute, and now the latest, the deceased serial killer seated in that dark cellar, surrounded by the shadowy figures of his victims, wailing in the dark.

There was something else, too. A blonde girl, young, mid-teens perhaps, begging him for help. She was standing in the cellar of the farmhouse, alone, afraid. The dark, moaning figures had circled her, and were reaching for her, tearing at her clothes, clawing at her skin. She shouted to him, pleading for him to save her, tears streaming down her cheeks. He had simply watched, ignoring her pleas.

This isn't my problem.

Then, suddenly, the young girl was not there; Charlie had taken her place. The sinister figures continued their grabbing, their pulling, snatching at her dark hair, groping her flesh. She screamed in terror, calling his name, shouting that he was the one that had gotten her into this.

This isn't my problem!

Charlie, too, was having a similarly restless night. She was in the living room of a small, neat flat, well maintained, clean. Not her type of décor, very feminine, the smell of lavender hanging in the air mingled with that of fresh coffee.

Charlie looked down at her hand, the large fist wrapped around a beer bottle. She saw that she was sat on a black leather sofa facing towards an old-fashioned box television of the type that she remembered from her early childhood in the nineties. The television was switched off; instead, entertainment was provided in the form of a nearby large stereo system, blaring out a song that she recognised by The Cranberries.

She felt relaxed, content, feeling like this warmth and comfort was something alien, new and novel, something that she had never before experienced.

A woman walked into the room clutching in one hand a steaming mug, in the other, a small box. She was strikingly pretty, dirty blonde hair, brown eyes, fantastic figure. Charlie smiled and felt her heart race upon seeing her, pleasant tingles running up her spine.

"I know it's not your birthday," She said, smiling sweetly, "But we got together just after your last one, so this is a sort of belated birthday present."

She handed over the small white box, which Charlie accepted reluctantly.

"Nobody ever gave me a gift before."

She opened the box. Inside, was a shining silver belcher chain. Charlie felt a lump in her throat. Another person spending their own hard-earned money to buy something for her *was unbelievable.*

"Let me put it on for you."

She stood, allowing the woman to wrap the chain around her neck, clasping it at the back.

Standing there, Charlie could see her reflection in the mirror. What she saw was a muscular man, wearing a white vest and blue jeans with combed-back dark hair and a scarred face, looking at her. His eyes were wide, staring, almost soulless. The gaze lingered for too long, almost as though the man in the reflection was studying her, trying to figure her out. Finally, a smile slowly spread across his face, and he winked.

Charlie, disturbed, pulled away her gaze, down towards her feet, when something caught her eye, sitting on the coffee table.

It was the crystal skull.

Sidney Taylor had once owned the skull.

SIX

Drake awoke at first light, feeling a frosty cold feeling in his fingers and toes, and with a terrible thirst. He almost felt hungover, feeling the same rough, uncomfortable feeling in his body that he would always feel in the mornings whilst on field training exercises with the Legion.

He climbed out of the van and took a brisk jog around the van a couple of times, to restore circulation and encourage his brain to awaken in line with the rest of his body. First order of the day would be water, then he would drive into town, find a café for coffee and hot food, before looking around for a room to rent, hopefully by the end of the day, to avoid another night in the van. Plus, he needed a shower. He knew that security work was out of the question in this area, due to this being McBride country, but he did still have a good amount of funds remaining from his last contract, and besides, he could advertise his "man with a van" services that was always good for bringing in quick cash. The next step once he had secured lodgings would be to locate an MMA gym, maybe he could even sort out some temporary work as an instructor there. Then, once settled in his new, temporary home, he could re-think his plans involving the skull, and Frankie. The ideal scenario would be to locate someone with links to Frank, as people with a connection always made the most promising hosts, but Frank was a man of few friends. Sure, there had been many associates, many colleagues, but what with Frank's tendencies to travel often and plant no roots anywhere, any people that became friendly with him were generally in, then out of his life again, briskly, as though they were simply walking by each other and slapping hands in a quick high five.

Of course, they often saw the same faces on the private military circuit, the same collection of misfits from various international military units such as the Russian Spetsnaz, the US Navy Seals and Delta Force, The British SAS and SBS, the Parachute Regiment, Royal Marines and of course, the French Foreign Legion from France. These men, however, were too much like himself and Frank to ever become emotionally attached to their colleagues. Yes, they had shared a beer or two over time, but all of them kept themselves cold and disconnected. Becoming upset when a colleague was killed was unprofessional; better to simply never become close.

That would be a problem for future Drake, he decided as he opened the rear door of the van in seek of water.

Inside, he identified the crate of water bottles, fumbled with the plastic and pulled out a bottle. Cold. As he drank, he stared into the back of the vehicle. There were bags in there, bottles of water, blankets…. But no Charlie.

He continued taking large gulps of the clear liquid, savouring the feeling of the coldness as it poured down into his gullet. He walked slowly around the exterior of the farmhouse, drinking, calling her name. When he received no form of reply, he stepped inside the door, called her again, catching that familiar odour of mould and stagnant water. After conducting a search of every room of the musky old building, including that bastard cellar, he concluded that she must have already left, without a goodbye. Rude. Realising that he was now alone in that haunted, cursed place, he felt a swift shudder of fear pass through his body, the image of the shapes in the darkness returning to his mind; the tormented victims.

Get a grip, Drakey boy. Breathe. Focus. They can't hurt you.

With a shrug, Drake returned to his van, happy to be away from that building again. If Charlie wanted to make her own way alone into town, on foot, then be that burden on her own shoulders. Perhaps if he drove back along the route that they came in, he would encounter the stroppy bitch along his way back into the town centre; then at least he could *offer* her a lift.

But she left her bags.

Why walk away without her bags? She didn't have his phone number, and he had no social media presence to speak of; he was not exactly easily contactable, he would be difficult to track down when she needed her clothes or wash bag, so the fact that she had disappeared without any of her earthly belongings less for the clothes on her back was slightly alarming.

It's on my head if anything happens to her.

He decided to wait in the van for a while. Perhaps she had walked to the garage for a bite to eat, gone for a walk or jog, or whatever else psychologically disturbed barmaids did with themselves at dawn.

You're getting soft on this one, Drakey.

"Shut up, Frank."

As Drake sat alone, he stared at the exterior of the abandoned ruin before him. Were those poor souls trapped there? Trapped in there with the spirit of the man that had caused their death and condemned them to that damp, dark, lonely shell? Imprisoned with their own tormentor, their own killer, mocking them?

He cleared his mind of dark thoughts, focusing on his breathing, and waited, sipping water, feeling his stomach grumbling impatiently. He needed some breakfast; he hadn't eaten a thing since that greasy cheeseburger the previous evening. And coffee, coffee really was a requirement. He waited thirty long, hungry minutes, took a piss against a nearby birch tree, waited another thirty minutes, then decided to leave. He could drive slowly, look out for her on the route.

If she goes missing, Drakey boy, you're the last one that she was seen alive with. And we all know you're a violent man. You were imprisoned in India for violent offences.

"Shut up Frankie." Drake muttered, switching on the ignition.

Glancing down at his hand, he caught sight of the silver ring on his index finger.

Shane spoke to me last night.

The knowledge that his Sensei was still out there, somewhere, still conscious in some form of afterlife, made Drake's spirit lift slightly. If not for the fact that he had dragged a barmaid across the country to a haunted farm and then lost her, he would have been feeling on top of the world right about now.

You lost the pretty barmaid, Drakey. This is why we can't have nice things.

But where exactly was Shane? Trapped in some shadowy reality, or in a utopia afterlife sipping divine wine and basking in the glory of the Gods? And where was Frank? If there was an otherworldly prison to punish the wicked, a hell, then Frank would surely be there. Shane, probably not. Frank, certainly. Was he burning in flames? Being tortured by terrible demons? Or wandering a dark, desolate landscape with other tortured souls, destined to remain there, joyless and forgotten, for eternity?

Wherever you are, Frank, I sent you there. I buried you in a lonely hole, then lied to your Mother's face, telling her that you had gone off in a crazed pursuit of some cursed skull that you had heard about from some crazy person. I told her that I had left you safe and sound in Chile, and that I had returned in search of regular work. I'm an asshole, Frankie. And I will keep seeking a way to bring you back from wherever you are trapped.

Drake tossed his empty water bottle onto the passenger's seat, then drove the van out, through the gap in the wall and onto the dirt road beyond, towards the main A road that led into town.

There was no sign of Charlie along the main road, the only living beings in sight being a couple of joggers and dog walkers, nor could he see a trace of her in any of the surrounding fields, or trees. Drake pulled into the garage to enquire with the attendant as to whether he had seen a girl fitting Charlie's description. The scrawny thirty-something had said that he hadn't, but by the way that he continued to tap away on his iPhone throughout their brief conversation without looking up once, Drake doubted as to whether this sack of shit would have even noticed her if she had walked in naked and taken a shit on his till.

"Thanks," he said to the ignorant attendant, "you've been a great help."

Drake drove on, through the industrial estate and then onto the high street, marginally busier than it had been during their drive through the previous evening, people on their way to work, pensioners out picking up as much shopping as they could physically carry, disinterested schoolkids walking slowly in groups towards their relative schools. Still, no Charlie. No tattooed, cocky barmaid.

He pulled into the first car park he saw after noticing an enticing greasy spoon café, deciding that he would be much more alert and productive after ingesting calories and caffeine. When hungry, Drake was irritable and impatient, which in turn caused him to lose focus as he thought of nothing but his stomach and its lack of content.

Drake described Charlie to the old dear in the café, asking her if she had seen a girl that looked like that entering or passing her café that morning. A friendly enough woman, but no use whatsoever. She stated that had she seen such a girl, she probably wouldn't have remembered.

He ate a plate of bacon and poached eggs, with a big black coffee; fuel for his search, whilst sitting by the window and monitoring the passing human traffic.

He bought a second, take-out coffee, then went for a drive around Thornham.

Thornham was a typical, impoverished Northern town, most of the employment provided by the minimum-wage factories on the industrial estate since the closure of the coal mine back in the late eighties. The high street had many shops that were no longer open; the victims of online shopping culture, and some of the pubs were now boarded up. Like most towns, Thornham did have a "nice" side of town in the form of a large estate of new-build houses, of which most of the inhabitants, Drake guessed, had taken advantage of the lower-priced houses in Thornham whilst commuting to the city for work. Thornham wasn't exactly what anyone would consider desirable, but Drake did look forward to cheap rent for a few weeks, even if he would be required to watch his back a little bit more when walking around these streets in the evenings. Drake, however, could take care of himself. Charlie, on the other hand, as tough as the girl appeared, was still a single girl wandering a strange town without any of her worldly belongings, or a vehicle, or even a roof to sleep under.

If I were Charlie, where would I go? Where does she like to hang around?

Bars. But perhaps not this early in the morning.

Cemeteries.

Right. Charlie had explained to Drake during her one-sided conversation on the drive to Thornham that whenever she wanted peace, she would visit a cemetery and find a quiet bench to sit on, as a cemetery seldom had large crowds, and also, is one of the few quiet places in the world where people tend to leave each other alone with their thoughts.

It took Drake around forty minutes to locate Thornham cemetery, after asking an elderly gentleman for directions. Luckily, the cemetery, a large, surprisingly well-kept estate, had its own car park. Useful, as he was carrying barely twenty pence in change and a selection of random foreign coins that he had passed from pocket to pocket every time that he had changed his jeans for the past year or so.

The cemetery *was* large, not as big as the vast war cemeteries that he had visited on remembrance days past, showing his respects for fallen fellow veterans, but still larger than most standard civilian plots used for depositing the dead.

Drake walked slowly between the stones, savouring the tranquillity and the sight of the carefully cut, bright green grass between the rows of monuments, his head glancing slowly left to right, looking carefully for signs of life. Any onlooker would have found that this large, battle-scarred apparition of a man dressed in black to be a strange sight, slowly and silently searching for something unknown amongst the graves. Drake, however, found not one trace of any onlookers. He saw not a single soul amongst the monuments to the dead; no mourners, no caretakers, no grave diggers.

Some of the headstones were beautiful. Black marble, white stone, carved angels, crucifixes. Some stones had photographs somehow printed onto their smooth surfaces, smiling, happy faces. Drake imagined those same faces now rotted, unsmiling, beneath the earth. Never to smile again, never to laugh.

You didn't even get a headstone, Frankie. Your mother can't even bring you flowers. She doesn't even know you're dead.

From that grim thought, Drake smiled as he imagined how Frank's face would have looked if anyone had ever actually bought him a bunch of flowers. He was never one for sentimentality.

He continued to look around, especially at the empty benches, strewn around the outside edges of the cemetery, beside the iron railings.

After ten minutes of walking, watching, he caught the sight of a huddled figure. It was the shape of a person, in a thick black jacket, seated on the grass, very still and silent, gazing solemnly at a grey headstone.

Drake could only see the rear of this silent figure; it was difficult to tell from his distance whether or not it was Charlie, or even if the sitting figure was male or female.

He walked towards this static shape, slowly closing the distance between them. As he approached, he could see a head of dark hair, short at the back, with the traces of a long fringe that could be seen blowing in the wind. It was Charlie.

She's alive. So relax.

Drake paused, for a moment contemplating leaving her there, alone with her own company. She had obviously visited the cemetery in order to be alone, to sit in silence. Had she wanted his company, then she wouldn't have come here.

She needs her stuff.

He sighed, then continued walking towards the girl, quietly. Once he had arrived at the spot, he sat beside her, not speaking, letting her ponder whatever it was that she needed to ponder. Perhaps the previous night had been an anti-climax. Perhaps she regretted travelling to Thornham, walking out on her job, her home. Perhaps she was just tired of Drake's company; he knew that he wasn't such a great joy to be around most of the time.

Charlie didn't look at him, nor did she acknowledge his presence. She simply sat, resting her forearms on her bent knees, staring unblinkingly at the headstone in front of her. Her expression appeared to be one of a mixture of anger and deep, deep sorrow. In her hand, she gripped the silver belcher chain, the chain that she claimed to have once belonged to Sidney Taylor.

Ash closed his eyes as he sat, cleared his mind. Cemeteries were a good spot for meditation, Charlie had been right. They were probably some of the most peaceful spots on earth. Most of the people there were six feet beneath the earth and silent, and as grim as a place created to dispose of the dead could be, it was still a beautiful green place decorated with flowers and art. It set a reminder that this was where everyone would end; silent and still. A reminder that life was to be lived. A glance at the inscriptions surrounding them further served to remind that death could come at any moment; so many of these people had been taken before their time.

Drake took some time to meditate, enjoying the ability to be in the company of another human being without the feeling of the need to ruin the peaceful silence with meaningless noise, however, he did need to find lodgings for the night and perhaps a bar, and so the matter at hand would soon need to be addressed.

"I have your stuff in my van, Charlie. Do you want me to leave you my phone number? You can collect it whenever you're ready."

Charlie slowly turned her head, her eyes locking onto his. Her expression looked different, intense. She blinked, blinked again, then frowned.

"Ash?"

Drake lowered his head and laughed.

"Have you been on the weed, Char? I've been here for twenty minutes or so."

She looked around, as though noticing her surroundings for the first time, her face a mask of bewilderment.

"How long have *I* been here?"

"I don't know, Charlie."

She continued to frown, looking around the cemetery once more, her eyes widening with confusion.

Charlie stood swiftly, wobbling slightly on her feet, then looked down at her clenched fist, at the silver clamped within it. Cramming the chain into her jacket pocket, she turned angrily to Ash.

"Did you fucking *drug* me?"

"What the fuck, Charlie? No! Of course not."

Drake also stood, tried to reach for her shoulders, calm her down, soothe her. She had clearly taken something, or maybe been drinking again, but whatever it had been, she shouldn't be walking around alone, especially with no home to go to.

"Don't fucking touch me!" She snapped, slapping away his hands.

Charlie turned her back to him and began hurriedly walking away, through the headstones. She wasn't staggering, Drake noticed, and he hadn't smelt any traces of alcohol, nor weed. Something stronger, then. Rohypnol?

Why would she take Rohypnol, Drakey, you fucking muppet?

He watched her marching away, seemingly heading towards an empty oak bench that sat twenty metres away, beside a large white gravestone in the shape of a praying angel.

I'll give her a minute, then walk over.

Drake waited at the same spot that they had been seated, giving Charlie some space for her brain to gather itself. He stretched his arms, yawning, absently glancing down to read the name carved onto the headstone that Charlie had been so intensely hypnotised by. The name on the stone was Nicola Donovan.

Drake had given Charlie a few minutes, smoking her cigarette on the bench, the bemused expression still souring her face.

When he finally approached and sat down beside her, she did not protest.

Charlie flicked away her still-burning cigarette butt, then without looking at him, spoke.

"Things have gotten really fucked up since you walked into my life, Ashton," She said, "I don't know who I am or where I am. I'm having vivid dreams that I'm someone else, dreams that I can't control. They're not good dreams, Ash."

She stared off into the distance, looking lost, helpless.

"Let's get somewhere to stay for the night. A hotel or a B and B. Then we can go to find something to eat. My treat."

Her head snapped around towards Drake, fixing him with an angry sneer.

"A hotel? With *you?*"

She turned away, shaking her head, laughing softly.

"I don't know who you are, Ash, but you're behind all this. And now you're following me. As much as I'm scared and confused right now, I think that what I need more than anything is to be as far away from you as possible."

Drake nodded slowly.

"Okay, Charlie. That's fine. But I only followed you because you walked away last night, or this morning, without your bags. I'm not here to hurt you."

"You took me to that farm, and you *did* something to me."

As much as he wanted to help her, make her safe, he knew that what she was saying was true. He *had* taken her to the farm as part of an experiment to try to work out how to unravel the mysteries of the skull; his end game being to reunite him with his brother. What he had done to this girl was unforgiveable; Had he simply drugged and raped her, that would have been a much kinder act that the horrors that he had actually subjected her to in that worm-ridden cellar.

Drake sighed, staring down at his samurai ring. Shane would be ashamed of what he had become. The honour that he for years had attempted to instil in the boys had fallen on deaf ears. He had grown into a violent killer, lacking conscience. He had murdered his best friend, lied to his best friend's mother. He had welcomed the soul of a brutal killer into the body of an innocent woman, all in the name of his equally immoral, murdering brother.

I'm such an asshole.

"Okay, okay," he said, resigned, "I'll back off and leave you alone. Do you want to get your bags now?"

"No."

"Then take my phone number, contact me when you get somewhere to stay, and I'll drop them off. Or we can meet somewhere."

Drake pulled a crumpled pile of business cards from the pocket of his jacket, passing one of them across to Charlie. She took the card, glanced at it.

Ashton Drake. Private Military Contractor. Close Protection. Hostile Environment. Maritime Security.

"And if you need anything, Charlie, please call me. You're right, I *am* a bad guy, but I try not to be. If you run out of money, need a place to stay, or even somebody to just have a drink with, please don't hesitate."

Charlie remained silent, gazing at the business card in her hand.

"And Charlie, did you notice whose grave that was?"

She looked at him, searching his face, waiting for an explanation.

"It was Nicola Donovan," he continued, "the girlfriend of Sid Taylor. Did you know where she was buried?"

Charlie looked for a moment like she was about to weep, as she continued to search Drake's face. Her expression then went from one of sadness to stern defiance, as she broke eye contact.

Then, placing the card into her inside jacket pocket, Charlie stood, and without another word, walked away, towards the exit.

SEVEN

Charlie was resting on an uncomfortable bed, staring at a white ceiling, listening to the tall, thin man that shared the room with her talking excitedly. She did not recognise the room; it was small, smaller than any of the bedsits or rooms in which she had ever stayed. She was lying on the top row of two bunk beds; in a room covered with tatty A4 sized pictures of bikini-clad women, clearly torn from the pages of men's magazines. The door to the room was a heavy-looking metal thing with a hatch for a window; the small window set into the wall had bars, deeply set into thick brick. A cell. She was in prison.
The tall, dark skinned, thin bald man that shared the cell with her was standing by her bed, talking excitedly. He was talking of ancient relics, the means to raise the dead, the ticket to eternal life and the power to switch between mortal bodies. He explained that he knew where to find one such magical piece, a crystal skull that had been passed from shaman to shaman for hundreds, maybe thousands of years. The man that currently held it, he had said, was a great Necromancer known by the name of Naja Haje.
Charlie looked at him, searching his face.
"And where, Aayush, can I find this man?"

Drake's day had been quite productive. Two days on from his conversation with Charlie in Thornham cemetery, and after two dull nights in a cheap B and B, he had firstly secured a room in a shared flat, sharing with a slightly overweight, bespectacled, middle-aged, long haired man named Marcus, the type of man who spent his weekends watching Lord Of The Rings and playing World of Warcraft whilst eating takeaway pizza. Drake didn't mind these types, they generally kept themselves to themselves, mixed in their own social circles, and didn't stress themselves attempting to ensure that they always had the most up-to-date hairstyles or shoes, and ignored societal norms. They weren't *his* type of crowd, if any crowd was, however they were generally harmless, friendly folk. They were often the subject of ridicule to loud, vanity-stricken morons that perceived anyone that dared to dress slightly different to the mainstream sheep to be outsiders that immediately deserved to be stoned to death. In Drake's opinion, Marcus was okay. He wouldn't ask questions, wouldn't focus his attention where it wasn't wanted, which was, namely, Drake's business.

Secondly, he had found himself some temporary employment as a bouncer in a small strip club for three nights a week, starting the following Thursday. The manager, a forty-something ex-soldier, was clearly impressed by Drake's CV, the two of them chatting at length about Drake's time in the 2nd Foreign Parachute Regiment out in Corsica. Drake had asked the man, known only as "Rusty", how he had managed to avoid the seemingly mandatory absorption of his club into the "protection" umbrella of McBride's security. Rusty had said that McBride appeared to have overlooked the place, perhaps because their clientele in the *Red Minx* were mostly made up of the regular, stereotypical dirty old men, with the occasional stag party passing through. Not much in the way of profit, even less, for McBride's crew, in the way of selling on their drugs, excepting for a few lines of coke here and there, perhaps, to the stag parties. The location, close to the railway line and away from the main strip of bars in the town centre, meant that most men who were out looking to see a pair of tits would go to the larger strip club in town after visiting the regular bars for their fill of their chosen tipple. Their regulars were the older factory workers living locally, who wanted nothing less than the downtown crowds when they were going out quietly to leer at the only sight of a naked girl that they would likely have for a long, long time.

As well as the regular doorman work, Drake had also advertised the services of himself and his van online, already receiving a request from a single mother wanting a second-hand fridge freezer collecting from an address that was selling the appliance. The petty cash would be flowing in nicely, slowing down the drain on his finances; the next step now would be to email his usual contacts on the PMC circuit to arrange the next contract, or even perhaps a little black market work, the type of work that generally came with a much shorter contract and a considerably higher payday.

Returning from the local convenience store with a ready cooked chicken, some salad and a few bags of fruit, Drake walked into the kitchen of the flat. Marcus was waiting by the microwave, watching the radioactive glow illuminating a burger that turned slowly inside. The two men greeted each other before Drake began to prepare his meal.

Marcus watched as Drake sliced off big hunks of chicken onto a plate before throwing on piles of the pre-prepared, bagged salad.

"Healthy!" He noted.

Drake nodded, a thin, forced smile on his lips.

The radio was playing in the background; local news. Drake placed his plate on the kitchen table, removed two of his beers from the fridge and, passing one to Marcus who accepted it gratefully, he sat, half-listening to the droning voice as he ate.

"The man has been identified as forty-nine-year-old Trevor Walters, who was known to police for a string of violent offences. Walters, who was a former member of the Blackhearts Motorcycle Club, was found by his partner, stabbed to death in his flat on King Alfred Road, Thornham."

"Marcus, turn that up!" Spat Drake, pieces of chewed chicken flying from his lips.

Marcus, looking alarmed, reached over and raised the volume on his little DAB radio, looking at Drake quizzically.

"Someone you know?" He asked worriedly. Clearly, Marcus was slightly concerned that his new flatmate may have potentially unsavoury connections. Marcus was *not* the type to be mixing with such people as Trevor Walters. Drake waved his hand irritably at him, beckoning him to silence.

The Blackhearts. Stabbed to death.

That fucker is still inside Charlie. Taylor. That piece of shit. He's making her kill people.

Drake closed his eyes, placing his head in his hands; he was completely out of his depth here. If Charlie was being led on some kind of vengeful rampage, hunting down the enemies of Sidney Taylor, then McBride would soon turn his beady eyes onto her. How far would one single girl get against a vast criminal network, a network of dangerous, violent sociopaths? Charlie, armed with a knife. And Drake felt that he was powerless to help her.

Powerless? Do you forget who you are, Drakey boy? Time to raise the black flag.

Frank was right. *Raise the black flag.* Frank's favourite saying. Whenever the situation became dangerous, whenever it came to the point that the two of them would need to bite the bullet and run headlong into the danger, whenever it was necessary to dole out some excruciating violence in order to survive, Frank's words always gave Drake that essential boost of adrenaline. *It's time to raise the black flag.*

I'm Ashton fucking Drake. I shit guys like McBride. I am one serious, dangerous badass. And I have absolutely nothing to lose.

He exhaled, relaxed. He knew what he had to do. It was time to raise the black flag.

"I'm sorry, Marcus," he said calmly, "I thought they were talking about someone else."

Marcus, looking satisfied with his answer, nodded, turning back to the microwave to remove his soggy cheeseburger from within.

Drake calmly finished his meal and washed up his plate. Then, still carrying his beer, he took his keys from the rack of hooks on the back of the kitchen door and left the flat. Time to raise the black flag.

Charlie was walking along a dark street, poorly illuminated by intermittent lamp posts, a run-down road lined with numerous businesses, most of which had closed for the evening; a betting shop, closed. A small off-licence, apparently open, but with its windows boarded up. A boxing gym, closed. A number of scantily-clad women in heavy make-up lurked along the street, walking seductively whilst staring at the occasional car that passed by slowly. There were some men, shady-looking, hanging back from the main path, smoking cigarettes in shop doorways, all staring at Charlie. She was very much out of place walking this street, this apparition in jeans and combat boots, walking alone in a place like this.

And how the fuck did I get here?

The last memory that Charlie could recall before finding herself on this strange, dark street had been of eating fried chicken and coleslaw in a small pizza restaurant, earlier in the day. She had clearly suffered another blackout; a recurring problem that had been happening ever since *that night,* in the farmhouse. The blackouts were becoming more frequent, and for longer periods; the frightening dreams were becoming clearer and more vivid. The dreams were of Sid's life, she *knew* that, he was trying to show her, make her *understand*, but this was scaring her, she had no control over her own life anymore. She didn't want this connection, not anymore. Charlie didn't even know how many days had passed since that night at the farm. How much time had passed during each blackout? What did she *do* during these blackouts? She certainly hadn't been lying down sleeping; on one occasion she had awoken in a bar, another time on a bus. On the bus, she had become particularly alarmed after finding a lock knife in the pocket of her jacket; she had pulled the thing out, wondering what the hard, heavy object within her clothing had been, then, realising that it was a weapon, had hurriedly hidden it back within the confines of the jacket before any of the other passengers noticed. She wasn't averse to carrying a weapon, but to find one on her person that she had never seen before was slightly alarming.

And now, she found herself walking this unfamiliar street full of unsavoury characters, a young woman, alone.

Charlie desperately tried to make some sense of her surroundings, checking each street sign, each building, hoping to find something, anything that she recognised. Her watch said ten fifty; soon, even the off-licences and other late-night businesses would surely be closing, less for perhaps the bars. Perhaps if she could find a bar with security, there would be at least some degree of safety within; these prostitute-littered streets were certainly far from safe.

I could call Ash.

Ash could find her, collect her, take her somewhere safe. Besides, he still had her bags. A change of clothes would be more than welcome right about now. Charlie still had on the same clothes that she had worn to travel to Thornham with Ash, how long ago that had been, she was not sure. Some of her money had been spent paying for a night in a bed and breakfast, however, after having a much-welcomed shower and then getting into bed, she had awoken at just after 3am in the garden of a residential property, finding herself looking through somebody's window into a dark kitchen within.

Charlie was afraid. Afraid of what was happening to her, afraid of what she had done during her long blackouts. She did need some help, and Ash was the only person who could understand.

But Ash is the one who caused all this. Whatever happened to me in that farmhouse is entirely down to him.

"Hey, Elvira! How much for a suck?"

A man's voice, calling from a dark side street, a residential street with a poorly maintained row of small terraced houses, one of which had, on its overgrown lawn, the stereotypical battered car without wheels, resting on a pile of bricks. A rough street, she deduced.

Oh god, why am I here?

The tracksuit-clad, hooded man had three similarly dressed associates accompanying him, laughing at his crude remark as the four of them approached her slowly, drinking from large cider bottles. They were around twenty metres away, Charlie guessed.

"Ask your friend," she replied, "he looks like he knows what he's doing."

Why did I respond? Why can I never just keep my fucking mouth shut?

Charlie continued walking with a slightly increased pace as the group, laughing like rabid hyenas, gradually closed the distance between them. Her heart began to thump heavily as the adrenaline surged through her body, preparing itself for the primal fight or flight. Charlie had always thought herself streetwise, and she was. This type of area at this time of night was not somewhere that she would ever allow herself to be, especially not alone; especially when she did not know any of the safe areas or the best escape routes, should something go wrong. She could certainly handle herself, and had indeed been forced to defend herself on many an occasion throughout all the worst years, especially in the Young Offender's detention centre, but against four men, possibly armed, an escape would be preferable, and also much wiser.

I should have walked into a shop and called Ash. He got me into this, he owes me.

The rows of shops and businesses had ended, and Charlie now found herself walking along an even darker row of town houses; there were no longer any other visible pedestrians around, unsavoury-looking or otherwise, less for the four approaching, hooded figures. She glanced back, over her shoulder and beyond the four idiots, to see if any of the hookers or lurkers that she had passed were close enough to hear her if she was forced to call for help; there was one woman visible, probably fifty metres or so away up the street, speaking to a man in a white hatchback, before climbing in. The car drove away, in the opposite direction. Nobody else was in sight. Charlie was alone. Turning around and walking back in the direction from which she had came, to the busier area with the open off-licence, was no longer an option; she would have to now cross paths with her pursuers in order to do that. She considered knocking on a door, but, judging the state of some of the houses, with windows covered up with wooden boards and graffiti sprayed across the walls and doors, she decided against it.

"When you see my dick, you'll be paying *me* to have a taste." More laughter. They were probably now ten metres away, Charlie estimated.

Ahead, she saw a space between the houses, clearly a pathway leading off the street to elsewhere. A possible escape route.

If I can turn into that gap, I can just run. I'll create some good distance between us before they realise that I'm running. As fast as possible into the darkness, they may not even see me escaping.

Again, her pace further quickened as she tucked her hand into her inside pocket, feeling the comforting, cold hardness of the knife within. If she felt that the situation required it, she would stick the blade into the closest one of her tormentors before making a desperate run for it. As she approached the gap that seperated the houses, now only a couple of metres away at her right-hand side, she again quickened her pace, then made a sudden, swift turn into the dark alleyway beyond.

Just as Charlie was about to sprint deep into the darkness, she felt an arm, a strong arm, wrapping around her neck as her attacker pushed her deeper into the alley.

"Don't you dare fucking scream, or I'll cut you."

She didn't scream. She didn't struggle. Charlie simply fell immediately into a dazed, paralysing trance, then everything went black.

Before becoming aware of her surroundings, she heard the noise. A banging, like something heavy striking against wood. Not a knock, but a loud crash, like a door was being kicked or struck with a large, blunt object. Charlie, shaken into alertness by the violent sound, saw that she was once again back in that tidy flat, the sweet-smelling little haven with the feminine touch.

"Nicky, lock yourself in the bathroom!" She called, again in that rough, male voice, "Go!"

The pretty blonde stood, frozen in shock in the hallway of the familiar flat, staring towards the door that was seemingly being smashed through. Male voices could be heard speaking at the other side of the door, conversing in words that could not be deciphered.

Charlie reached down, beneath the sofa cushion, feeling the handle of the hunting knife that she somehow found very familiar and comforting, and grasped it tightly. She ran towards the woman, wrapping her thick, muscular arms around her waist and pulling her backwards, away from the door and whoever was trying to enter.

The woman came suddenly alive then, screaming and struggling. She resisted, attempting to pull free, calling out loud.

"Sid! Sid!"

"Nicky! It's me!" She shouted to her.

Charlie threw the young woman (Nicky? Nicola?) roughly into the bathroom, seeing her stumble and fall on her hands and knees to the floor with a cry, causing a sudden, sickening pang of guilt within her stomach. That had been necessary; there would be time for apologies later, if they both survived this.

The door then flew inwards, crashing into the wall of the narrow hallway. A large man, shaven-headed and bearded, wearing a black leather jacket, charged angrily towards Charlie. (Sid?)

With surprising speed and agility, despite her large frame, Charlie found herself lunging forwards, stabbing the man in the chest, then with graceful footwork, stepping back swiftly, avoiding a swinging punch from a meaty fist, then, when the man was slightly off-balance, leaping forwards again, stabbing him repeatedly in the chest, the neck, wherever the blade connected. The skinhead wheezed, a sound like air being released from a balloon, and his eyes widened, looking into hers. She stepped back again as the man tumbled forwards, hitting the floor face-first in a torrent of gushing blood.

Charlie growled, a sinister, threatening snarl, as another man followed the first, a machete raised in one hand. This one wore the distinctive sleeveless leather jacket, the "cut", of The Blackhearts MC.

Charlie jumped back into the living room, narrowly avoiding a downward swing of the huge blade. As the biker raised the machete to strike again, she stepped in close, grabbed the man at the back of the head by his long hair and plunged the blade of the hunting knife into his jugular. She watched his eyes widen in shock, savouring the fear displayed in his expression, then she removed the knife and stabbed again, and again, in the neck and upper chest.

By then, there were several other men shoving their way into the living room. Charlie dropped the dying biker, stepping back and raising the blade again to defend herself. There was a man to her left, one to her right, and two approaching from the front. All were armed, one with a baseball bat, one with a thick metal bar and one holding a handgun, aimed directly at her face with a steady hand. The older man, standing back slightly, a thin, wiry, angry-looking man, long haired and bearded, held a blowtorch.

"Hello, Taylor." He said, grinning, "Did you think you could just carve up my boys and walk away?"

"Your guys, McBride, yes." She replied, swinging the knife at the nearest man, who was approaching slowly with his bat. The blade passed the man's neck by an inch as he stepped back quickly to avoid having his throat sliced; simultaneously, Charlie felt a sharp blow to her head from the opposite side, sending a blinding white flash across her vision as her head began to spin. Dazed, she swung the knife sharply in every direction, feeling the blade connect with something solid, hearing a cry of pain and anger. The blows continued, striking her left arm, which was raised to defend against the torrent of blows, and her head. She continued swinging the knife, occasionally striking something or someone, until after a few seconds, when she found herself collapsed to the floor beneath the rains of hard blows, without having another ounce of strength to fight through the overwhelming dizziness.

"Stop hitting him," She heard the older man's voice say, "I want him to feel this for as long as possible before the bastard goes into shock. Hold him down."

Charlie was laid on the thick carpet, sticky with blood, motionless, seeing, on the floor beside her and spattered with crimson, the crystal skull. A thick hand reached down, picked it up.

"Hey, look at this," he said, "I'm taking this thing."

Two of the men knelt at either side of her, holding her in place by kneeling on her legs and placing their upper bodyweight down onto her shoulders and arms.

McBride approached, the blowtorch held in one hand, alight. The other man, a greasy-looking one-eyed character with dark features and a thick moustache, continued pointing the gun down at her.

"Eddie, go and search the house. I heard a bitch screaming. Make sure she doesn't escape. You can snuff her when we're done with Taylor here. No fucking, though. Unfortunately, we don't have time."

Grinning with malice, McBride then brought the burning blowtorch down, towards her face.

Charlie's breaths were heavy, her hands shaking. Perspiration dripped from her brow, into her eyes, the salt causing them to sting. She felt hot and sweaty; her heart was racing, almost like she had just stepped off a treadmill. Looking around, she saw that she had returned to reality, again back in control of her body, but whereabouts she now was, Charlie was not sure. Her surroundings were dark, unlit, a red brick wall at either side of her covered in crude graffiti.

Catching her eye, at her feet on the concrete floor, a movement. Something large and dark was slowly crawling on the litter-strewn tarmac, breathing in gurgles. Charlie jumped in shock, clenching her fists and teeth, gasping out loud.

What the fuck?

Blinking, adjusting her eyes, Charlie saw that the shape was a human, a hooded, male-looking figure in tracksuit trousers and a hoodie. He was attempting to crawl away from her, quite clearly injured, dragging one leg behind him, as though it were broken.

Another noise, a man, coughing, behind her. Charlie turned her head, saw another man, similarly dressed, attempting to crawl to his feet.

She felt her jacket, the familiar feel of the lock knife. Reaching inside her jacket, she pulled it out, opening the blade and pointing it towards the wheezing man who was attempting to stand.

It's those assholes who attacked me. Where are the other two?

"Hey fuckhead!" She said, kicking him hard in the stomach, causing him to retch, doubling over in pain, "what happened here?"

"Please stop." He croaked, "Please no more."

"Stop *what?*"

"Please..."

This is fucking insane.

Charlie kicked the punk one more time, this time in the face, then turned to his companion, still crawling away up the alleyway. She took two steps towards the broken-legged man and delivered two powerful kicks to his stomach.

"Fucking *pricks!* Threaten to cut me? How about I fucking cut *you?*"

Charlie clutched the knife in one trembling hand, momentarily considering sticking these bastards with it. Deciding finally that time again behind bars was not an attractive prospect, she then hurried away, down the alleyway, contemplating again whether to call Ash for help. She certainly wasn't the damsel-in-distress type, had never asked a man for help in her life, however, something strange and frightening was happening to her, caused by him and his fucking skull; the only person that may be able to shed some light on these occurrences, unfortunately, was that miserable, dead-serial-killer-raising bastard.

The two bouncers standing outside of the club stared blankly at Drake as he approached. The queue for entry was sectioned against the wall by a metal fence, the row of rowdy party seekers around twenty thick. The doormen watched as Drake walked straight towards the front, clearly concerned that this big lone weirdo was thinking of attempting to jump the queue.

"Hi guys, how are you doing?" He said, putting on his best, amiable nice-guy act. Obviously, the men were suspicious, and also didn't themselves seem the talkative types; Drake, with his large build, scarred face and shortly-cropped hair, looked like them, a typical heavy, an enforcer. These two bouncers looked like the stereotypical thug; both heavily-set, with bald heads, wearing black bomber jackets.

We always had much more finesse than these doorman types, Drakey boy. We ate men like these for breakfast.

The pair of them, unsurprisingly, ignored Drake's friendly greeting.

"Get to the back of the line, pal." The larger of the two said, his scowling expression unchanging, as his partner turned away to look down at the backside of a scantily-clad young girl of whom he had just granted entry inside, his leer lingering as she walked into the neon-lit darkness within. The girl, to Drake, certainly didn't look as though she were old enough to be walking in there.

"Oh, I'm not coming in," Drake replied, his eyes scanning the building and the queue of people lining up along the wall, "I'm just having a look at the place."

The smaller of the pair had turned his attention away from the girl and back towards Drake, and the two doormen then looked at each other in an expression that may have been quizzical, had either of them had any other expressions except for their one generic frown.

"Who the fuck are you?" Said the big one, looking again at Drake.

"My names Armand." He replied, using his given French name, the name he used in the Legion, as he held out his hand, offering a shake.

"Okay, Armand," Said the smaller one, "you can fuck off now."

"Get in the queue," interrupted the larger man, quickly, "Or go away. We're busy."

Drake pulled his hand away, smiling in amusement. McBride's goons here on this door were really the bottom of the barrel. Looking a lot like an enforcer, Drake could easily have been a thug from a rival organised crime group, carrying out a reconnaissance of enemy territories, checking their defences. Had he been in the position of these bouncers, Drake would have feigned friendliness, tactfully taking a photograph on his phone of the stranger, asking him as many questions as possible. In cases of extreme suspicion, he would have invited him inside for a free drink, then taken him into the office to discover his true purpose for checking out the premises.

These are amateurs, Drakey. They shouldn't be any trouble. Time to raise the black flag.

"I'm actually enquiring about a job. I'm new in the area, a doorman by trade." Drake said, still smiling, still keeping up the act.

"We don't need any staff." The larger one. The smaller of the two, although "small" was not a word that anyone would use to describe this man, was shifting his weight from foot to foot, grinding his teeth and staring at Drake, unblinking.

"Are you sure? You work for John McBride, don't you? Me and him go *way* back. We used to burn people's faces off together. Good times."

Drake turned his eyes towards the angrier-looking bouncer, looking anxious and agitated with what Drake perceived as *roid rage*, a short fuse caused by imbalanced hormones caused by the consumption of steroids. He had met so many bouncers in his time that suffered from this self-inflicted affliction. Their eyes locked, the two men staring at each other for several seconds. It became apparent that Drake smiling directly at his face was making the grumpy doorman's anger deepen, so he decided to continue staring, finding a degree of entertainment in watching this moron getting himself all worked up.

"I Think you should fuck off now," said Large, looking over at his partner, "Steve here is getting upset."

"That's cute. But I don't want to upset anyone. I just need to speak to management. I personally don't think you two are the people who are capable of dealing with recruitment; or anything that involves reading or writing, for that matter."

Large waved more people through, many of which who were now watching with interest as the stranger in the black military jacket was seemingly attempting to get a rise out of the door staff. They were hoping to have their night livened up by watching someone receive a kicking.

Suddenly, the smaller man spoke, his voice a decibel higher than it had been previously.

"I'll take you to see management," He said, irritably, "Let's go through the staff entrance."

"It speaks!" Called Drake, raising his face and hands to the sky, "It's alive! Who put fifty pence in *you*?"

The chunky man's face, *Steve*, flushed with anger as he pushed open the nearest fence link, before hurriedly stepping out onto the street. His legs were out of proportion to the rest of his body, thinner by far than his upper torso. His arms, Drake noticed, chuckling softly to himself, were thicker than his thighs.

"Follow me."

He walked around the side of the large building, to the rear, passing a row of overflowing bins, with Drake following close behind.

"Slow down, you'll have a heart attack." He mocked, seeing the bouncer's shoulders visibly tense as he heard Drake's voice.

Oh, I'm really going to get it now.

The rear of the club was enclosed by a high wall. At the back was what appeared to be a tradesman's entrance for deliveries, next to which was stacked piles of black bin bags, emanating the stench of decay. Stacks of empty beer bottle crates sat beside the bins, through which Drake could see rats crawling, content in their plastic palace beside an ample food source.

The two men began to walk into the enclosed space, when Drake acted. He struck the chunky doorman hard in the side of the neck, with the ridge of his hand, causing him to croak loudly, his hand reaching up towards the spot upon where he had been hit. He turned, wide-eyed, to look towards his attacker, who jabbed him with a closed fist onto his nose, splitting it with a loud popping noise, followed by a small spurt of blood. The intent was not to knock the man out, simply to stun. Drake needed to keep him awake for a while yet.

The bouncer was shocked and still gasping for breath, and yet he still threw a punch, perhaps an automatic response, a clumsy haymaker that Drake caught easily before using his right leg to sweep his attacker onto his back. The drop down to the concrete caused another loud gasp, not, however, loud enough to alert anyone within the club, all deafened by the thumping dance music.

Drake, keeping hold of the arm that he had grabbed, stepped over the doorman's head with his left foot, digging his booted heel into his neck as he pulled the man's arm upwards and across his right knee, holding him there in a painful arm bar whilst simultaneously placing pressure on the neck.

"You fuck…" Croaked the floored man, "You're a fuck.."

"Yes I am. I'm a fuck."

"I'll fucking.. I'll.."

"I'll tell you what you'll do. You'll tell me where I can find McBride."

"Fuck.."

Drake sighed, before carrying out the act that he had known would be inevitable. He bent the trapped arm in the wrong direction, pulling hard until he heard a sickening *crack*. The bouncer on the floor screeched in agony, thrashing and writhing. Drake kept the man trapped between his legs, still gripping the trapped arm, allowing him a few moments to register what had just happened to his arm.

"You fucking fuck! You fuck!"

"We know I'm a fuck. We already established that. That wasn't what I asked. Now, I can work on your other arm, then your legs, or you can tell me where I can find McBride."

Drake pulled out his small knife from his side pocket, opening the blade with his thumb. He pressed the sharpened side against Steve's hand, drawing it across the outer side, slicing into the skin and watching the blood pour. The unfortunate doorman shrieked again, repeatedly calling Drake a "fuck."

"We can do this all night, Steve. Or you can tell me what I need to know, and I can let you enjoy the rest of your life. You won't be doing any bench press for a while, mind. Maybe you could get on a leg press machine. I'd recommend it."

"He's usually, he's usually…" Steve began, before crying out in pain once more, his face wincing.

"Steve, you had better hurry up, or I'll *really* give you something to cry about. I've barely touched you yet. Man the fuck up."

Steve had stopped struggling and was now sobbing, tears streaming down his cheeks, his face scrunched up in a pained grimace, reminding Drake of a bulldog.

"His office in his car wash on station road," he said in a pained, high-pitched voice, "That's where he does most of his business. In his portacabin there!"

"Are you lying to me Steve? If you are, I'll be back when you're not expecting it. Maybe when you're taking a shit, or in the shower. I'm not a man to be fucked with, Steve. I killed McBride's little fuck buddy Walters in his flat last night. If you don't want the same fate, do *not* fuck with me."

"I'm not fucking lying!"

"Okay."

Drake let the arm drop, watching Steve cradle it, curling into a foetal position as he hyperventilated.

"You lot really are fucking amateurs."

Drake then sat himself down beside the man, producing his hip flask from within his jacket and unscrewing the lid. He took a sip, rinsing out his mouth with the taste of the good Scotch within. He then held the flask out, towards Steve's mouth.

"Take some." He said, shaking the little bottle slightly.

Steve took it with his good hand, trembling uncontrollably, and brought it to his quivering mouth. He took two big gulps, then held it back towards Drake, never once making eye contact.

Drake took the flask, then with his free hand, patted the big man on the shoulder twice, affectionately. The guy was a bit of a shit, but still, no pleasure had been gained from hurting him like that.

"Thanks, Steve. I'm sorry for what I had to just do."

"McBride is fucking dangerous," Steve said, the colour now drained from his round face, "he *will* kill you."

"That's cute."

"So who the fuck *is* this cockroach? Is he a Blackheart?"

McBride was seated at his desk, staring menacingly at his head of Security for the *Rio*, the premier night spot in Thornham town centre, a troubled establishment, like most of the clubs and bars that he "protected", rife with narcotics and violence. McBride's face was fixed with an expression even more twisted with hate and rage than was usual as he stared down the nervous employee, strumming his fingers impatiently at his desk. Eduard stood at his side, the Albanian's one eye also burning into the terrified head doorman, who was shakily sipping at the beer bottle that McBride had given to him from the stash in his mini fridge in the corner. Another thug, a small, clean-shaven, neat looking young man, professional-looking with a straight gait, stood calmly and quietly beside the exit.

"I don't know who he is; Mikey said that he was quite a big guy with facial scars. Never seen him before. I can show you the CCTV back at the club, his face isn't very clear, mind."

"And what about that fat useless bastard, what was his name?"

"Steve."

"Steve. I need to see him. Tell me what he said to Steve."

The terrified security manager, a big-bellied former boxer that people called Swifty, was looking from Eddie to McBride, and back again. Swifty had worked at *Rio* prior to McBride taking over the security contract; McBride had decided to let the man keep his job as Swifty had managed the security of the place for fifteen years; he knew all the bar staff, they trusted him. Sometimes it would keep business running a little more smoothly when the staff's point of contact for security was a familiar face, as opposed to McBride's intimidating thugs, most of whom had the people skills of a rabid hyena. McBride had since, however, regretted his decision in keeping this waste of space in employment, deciding that Swifty had turned out to be cowardly, a weasel. He would always stand behind his doormen whenever trouble arose, preferring to hide in the security office chatting to his CCTV operatives, and constantly seemed to be shitting in his pants whenever he was called into the office.

"Mr. McBride, I'm very sorry for how the boys handled this…"

McBride threw his own beer bottle, hard, over Swifty's shoulder, smashing it against the wall. Swifty felt droplets of beer and small shards of glass peppering the back of his thick neck and head as he tensed up, closing his eyes and preparing for the worst.

"THAT IS *NOT* WHAT I FUCKING ASKED YOU!"

McBride was on his feet now, leaning over his desk. His wild eyes were inches away from Swifty's face, close enough for his hot, foul-smelling breath to be felt upon his skin.

"Mr McBride… Steve tells me that he took this man around the back of the club to teach him a lesson. He was taunting the door staff. Then the man attacked him, and then admitted to killing your friend Walters."

"He really taught him a fucking lesson, didn't he?" Mcbride growled, moving his face even closer, "So, what did he say about *me?*"

"Nothing, Mr. McBride."

The old man closed his eyes and slowly lowered himself to his seat. Swifty could see him muttering something inaudible, his lips moving without words.

"Mr. McBride, listen…"

McBride's eyes snapped open again, and suddenly, his hand appeared from under his desk, brandishing a revolver, aiming it directly at Swifty's mouth.

"One more fucking word out of that mouth and I will empty every round from this gun into it. I'll shoot off every single one of your teeth." His tone was low, and yet somehow, even more menacing than his shouting. Swifty's mouth remained open, but silent. His eyes were fixated on the barrel of the revolver, inches from his face.

"And one more thing, Swift. You DO NOT fucking tell ME to *LISTEN*! YOU DO NOT, *EVER*, TELL ME WHAT TO FUCKING *DO*!"

Swifty, unsure as to whether he was supposed to respond to this comment or not, remained silent, his mouth still agape, eyes almost as wide as his mouth. He was quite certain that he would die that night; he just hoped that McBride wouldn't be getting out the blowtorch, the terrible stories of which he was more than familiar with. He had never wanted to work for this man, however he had been too afraid to leave.

McBride again sat back, leaning back in his seat and breathing deeply. In his older years, he had been attempting some exercises with which to control his temper; the last thing that he wanted on the dawn of his retirement was to suffer a stroke or a heart attack in a tiny portacabin whilst beating down some incompetent cockroach. Calmer, he opened his eyes and again addressed his overweight employee.

"Swifty," he said, calmly placing the revolver atop his desk, "I am not asking you whether your waste of space doorman *told* this man where to find me; I know that the answer would be a *lie*. Perhaps not a lie from yourself, but certainly a lie from Steve. All that I ask is, did this piece of shit *ask* Steve where he could find me?"

"Yes, boss, he did."

McBride again closed his eyes. Swifty could see the old man's fists clenching tightly atop the desk, his knuckles turning white. He was very clearly burning with rage, and yet his hands were steady, his breathing slow and steady.

"Then he knows where to find me," McBride said slowly, eyes still shut, "Eduard, I'd like you to wait here. Shoot anybody that enters. Get rid of the body and I will pay your usual rate, plus a little extra if it turns out to be the cockroach who is apparently out looking for me."

McBride then opened his eyes and stared straight at Swifty. Swifty, still trembling, was covered in cold, sticky perspiration as he waited silently for his verdict feeling like a criminal in the dock awaiting sentence. Would he be sentenced to death? Or worse? This violent old bastard before him terrified him, indeed he terrified the entire criminal underworld. He was not famous for his mercy.

"Swift... I'm on the brink of retiring. Do you know why I use this office? I have bigger, more comfortable, lavish offices in various other businesses I own, and yet I choose this little portacabin at a car wash. Do you know why?"

"No, Mr. McBride."

"Of course you don't. You're a fucking monkey on a spaceship. You press the buttons that you've been trained to press, without having a clue what the fuck you're actually doing. I, on the other hand, own that spaceship. I'm the captain. The reason that I use this office is because it is the last place anyone would expect me to use to do my business. I'm not a man who needs home comforts, Swifty. I was in an MC for many years, I've done time behind bars, I've spent a lot of time sleeping on the floors of garages, in the back of vehicles, and not once did it bother me. Using a portacabin for business is comfortable enough for me. But now, now I want to retire. I'm getting a little old. Now, I think I *want* to start enjoying some luxuries. But I made a mistake. I don't make *many* mistakes, but this was a big one. I let too many of the fucking monkeys know where the captain's office was. I used this office too much. I brought lower-rung monkeys into my office to give them instructions, all because I like to *see* these fucking monkeys, read their faces and see if I can *trust* them. Your fucking... *Steve*... was one such monkey. Now, I wish that I could deal with this right now, but I need to relocate. Get out of my fucking sight, get that CCTV onto a disc, and I'll call you when I am ready to look at your ugly fat face again without feeling a deep urge to melt it off."

Swifty remained seated, unsure as to whether to stand up and leave, say thank you, or to simply wait until he was told exactly what to do. In the end, he decided on the latter. McBride stood, retrieving his firearm from the desktop. He nodded across to Eddie, then turned his attention to the small younger man by the door.

"Jack, bring the car around."

Jack nodded, then turned and moved towards the exit.

McBride looked down at his frightened-looking head of security, bemused at the open-mouthed, blank stare that was covering Swifty's face.

"Well?" McBride said with a smile, opening his arms wide, "Fuck off!"

Swifty, like a frightened rabbit, scrambled quickly to his feet and hurried towards the door.

"Yes, Mr. McBride."

Jack opened the door facing onto the dark, empty car wash beyond, and began to walk down the three wooden steps that led down from the portacabin door. He pressed the key fob of McBride's Jaguar, hearing the familiar beeping, then paused. There was a black VW Transporter van, parked right there in the car wash, sitting directly beside the shiny new Jag.

Jack scowled, confused for a split second. He decided that the best course of action would be to turn back and stop Mr. McBride from exiting his office until this vehicle had been investigated and the premises searched, but before he could make another move or sound, the blow was received. From behind the door of the portacabin the figure appeared, punching Jack's jaw with a powerful right hook that knocked him backwards, causing him to stumble dizzily, tumbling off of the stairs. He hit the gravel floor with a loud crunch, his jaw shattered.

Next out came a bewildered, frightened-looking fat man, hurrying through the door, panicked, as though running away from a rabid dog. He momentarily paused when he saw Drake, the bewilderment turning into a frown. The fear and confusion caused by whatever had scared him back inside the portacabin was being multiplied by the presence of this muscular, scarred, intense-looking man who had apparently just knocked out his colleague for no obvious reason. Following on behind the fat man came a one-eyed, greying man with dark features, with one eye socket on his face being an empty black void, his single eye pale and emotionless. The one-eyed man pushed his fat associate to one side, causing him to trip over the wooden stair and land onto his hands on the rough gravel. He then raised with his other hand a Glock handgun, bringing it up to bear onto Drake's chest. Drake acted quickly, with the back of his fist, he almost unconsciously knocked the gun hand aside, a shot ringing out and ricocheting from the stones below. Drake stepped forward, striking him with a headbutt to the face whilst simultaneously grabbing the wrist of the gun hand. Then, keeping hold of the wrist and keeping the barrel of the weapon pointed away from himself, he stepped back slightly and kicked the man hard to the chest, sending him crashing backwards back inside of the portacabin, leaving the handgun clutched within Drake's grip.

Raise the black flag.

The fat man had climbed to his feet and was now running, as fast as his heavy load would allow him. Drake let him go. This man would have no idea as to who Drake was, nor would he have the slightest clue as to where his boss was about to be taken. He could describe Drake, for certain, but that was of no concern. Drake watched him waddling away for a second; these were the kind of men he was dealing with.

Fucking amateurs.

Turning his attention back to the task at hand, he raised the handgun, stepping back from the cabin. The one-eyed man stood, a revolver now in his hand that he had obviously located from somewhere within the portacabin.

Drake fired a single shot, deliberately missing the mark, inches from Eduard's good eye.

"Don't move," Drake said, calmly but forcefully, "and throw me the gun."

Eduard froze, glaring with his one good eye at Drake, clearly trying to weigh up his odds. Could he bring the revolver up and fire before being shot down himself? How fast was this man? Eduard knew that he was quick, but how quick was this stranger? Was it worth his life to protect McBride? No, it wasn't. But would this man let him live if he allowed him to take McBride? Or kill him anyway?

"Throw me the fucking gun." Drake spoke calmly, coolly.

Let this old bastard realise who exactly is in control here.

Eduard did as he was told, tossing the silver revolver, which landed with a clunk in the gravel beside Drake's boots. Drake, keeping his eyes on his enemy, slowly lowered himself to retrieve the revolver with his free hand.

"Good man. Now exit the cabin. Both of you."

Eduard looked down at something, or someone, out of sight beside the door.

McBride, of course.

"NOW!"

Eduard raised his hands slowly and begrudgingly, walking slowly towards Drake, without breaking eye contact.

"You'll fucking regret this you piece of shit. You have no idea who you're fucking with here."

An Eastern European accent. Romanian? Albanian?

"That's cute. Hurry up. You too, McBride."

Eduard stepped forwards, onto the gravel, looking Drake up and down with a sneer of pure contempt screwing up his face.

He's looking for a chance. Waiting for me to slip up. Good luck with that.

Drake, as soon as Eduard was slightly beyond reaching distance, stepped suddenly forwards, swinging his arm up and bringing it down sharply in an arc, the thick metal of the heavy revolver cracking across the one-eyed thug's skull. Eduard stumbled backwards, and Drake followed, bringing the handgun down once again, harder, causing Eduard to drop to his knees, then onto his back awkwardly, half of his body sprawled on the lowest wooden step, half on the gravel. His hands raised up, touching the wound, feeling the blood running between his fingers.

He would be too dazed now to be a threat for a while.

Stepping back and raising the barrel again to aim it towards the door, Drake called out again.

"McBride, you step out now, or I throw a fucking grenade in there."

Of course, he didn't have a grenade. McBride very likely didn't believe that he did. Whether he would risk himself by taking that chance would be a very different question. Three seconds passed, then the man finally appeared, smiling bitterly. An old man. Long grey hair, grey beard, as thin as a rake. He looked like a crazed, crack-addicted Gandalf.

"*You're* John McBride?"

"The one and only."

Eduard sat alone in the darkness, within the confines of the portacabin. He had awoken from his semi-unconsciousness with a bitch of a headache and an immense swelling around his empty eye socket, making him for the first time grateful that there was no eyeball within. Upon regaining his alertness, Eddie had found himself bound tightly by his wrists and ankles with thick cable ties. The stranger had taken McBride and young

Jack Nichols away to an unknown destination, leaving Eduard closed inside the portacabin with the lights switched off.

Eduard was a man that did not forget faces. The visage of very man that he had ever met, worked with, fought or killed was burned deep into his subconscious. Names he occasionally struggled to recall, but faces, never.

And yet he had never seen that motherfucker in his life; that motherfucker who had *dared* to show up tonight and put his hands onto one-eyed Eddie. No doubt he was some enforcer from an up-and-coming gang wanting to make their reputation by bringing down the notorious McBride dynasty, just as Eduard had assisted McBride himself on his own bloody rise to power, wiping out an entire chapter of The Blackhearts followed by every other organised crime group across three counties. One-eyed Eddie, of course, was a freelancer; he had never officially been a member of McBride's vast criminal empire; Eduard was paid muscle, a gun for hire, the best in the business. McBride had known this and had desperately wanted the deadly Albanian as his right-hand-man. Eduard had told the biker that he did not tie himself down, that he belonged to nobody. To his credit, McBride had respected this, but still had continuously thrown money his way to keep him by his side and to keep him continuing to murder his enemies almost around the clock. Eduard also had his own small network of loyal killers, rendering his services even more sought after; McBride was constantly paying off Eduard's men so regularly that it made almost no difference whatsoever that the men did not belong to McBride. This fact did not bother Eduard in the slightest; all he cared for was his own integrity. He could hold his head high and still say that he was self-employed and freelance, that he had his own team of employees. Besides, working predominantly for one trusted client made his chances of being double-crossed significantly lower.

And now, Eddie had two choices; the first choice would be to walk away from McBride, seek other work, which could easily be found; whoever was hunting McBride clearly had no interest in Eddie, Eddie had simply been beaten and tied up after getting between the big guy and his quarry. The second option would be to seek vengeance, try to find McBride, to get his men together and rub from the face of the world every man involved in this insult. This latter option right now seemed the much more appealing prospect to the bound and gagged Albanian sitting on a cold floor with a split forehead. This attack may have een aimed at McBride and not at himself, however he still had a reputation to maintain. His own men even would lose respect for their feared and brutal leader if he allowed nobodies to pistol-whip him, restrain him and walk away. He could not allow this humiliation to go unavenged. But first, he would need to find a way to free himself and then make some phone calls.

Eduard shuffled on his backside, across to the desk, the outline of which his eye, slightly adjusted to the darkness, could identify. Once at the desk, he lifted his bound hands, finding the sharp corner of McBride's wooden desk; he then carefully placed his face against this corner, using it to gradually push down the gag that had been tied tightly to his mouth. Where the material for this gag had originated, Eduard guessed to be a cleaning cloth used by the car wash staff, judging by the dampness and the car wax smell upon it. The word "staff", of course, was a loose term; Eduard himself had personally trafficked these people into the country in order to provide them to McBride as slave labour. Referring to slaves as "staff" was rather misleading, to say the least.

Once the gag had been pushed down across his chin, Eduard breathed deeply, finally able to enjoy the comfort of being able to suck in oxygen through a mouth opened wide, as opposed to his stuffy nose.

Eduard took a few moments to breathe, deciding that his next step would be to use the edges of the desk to wear away the plastic of the cable ties that bound him. He had taken only three inhalations when he heard the steady footsteps approaching from across the gravel. A slow series of crunches, gradually growing in volume. Somebody was coming. Was it the stranger, returning to finish him off? Or a friendly face, an employee of McBride's empire? More likely the latter. Had the stranger wanted him dead, then surely, he would have already rendered Eddie cold. Or perhaps, he had later decided that it was better to leave no witnesses breathing, and so returned to permanently silence the man that could identify him? But Eduard hadn't heard the van returning. Any vehicle driving onto the crunchy gravel always made a considerable amount of noise; not even a pedal cycle could approach the portacabin stealthily, which was why McBride liked to surround his office with the noisy stones. The stranger must have pulled onto the gravel in his van whilst McBride was screaming at Swifty; how none of them had heard it was a mystery. Eddie manoeuvred himself quickly back to the dark corner of the cabin, deciding that he would prefer to identify anyone that may enter before he revealed his own presence. He climbed to his feet, pushing himself up against the wall for assistance; he may have been bound by his wrists and ankles, but nothing would prevent One-eyed Eddie from fighting to his last breath if it became necessary.

The footsteps came closer, the crunching of gravel replaced by the sound of heavy footwear upon the wooden steps, a slow, purposeful tread. The door opened, and a large-framed figure stepped inside. Eduard stared, for a moment believing that he was hallucinating, a vision caused by the head trauma that he had received, then after the vision had registered properly in his brain, he screamed.

Standing there in the doorway, was a man whose death Eduard had assisted with, twenty-three years earlier. The man looked exactly as he had after himself, McBride, Walters and Kuklinski had left him stone dead on the living room floor of that barmaid's flat. His jeans and t-shirt were covered in dried blood; his dark combed-back hair soaked in sweat and blood with long strands hanging down over his face, if that could even be described as a face. What had once been a face had gone. Where there should have been skin, a nose and lips, there remained a blackened, smoking, grinning skull. McBride had burnt away all of the man's features slowly with his signature blowtorch, taking great joy in scraping away the burnt flesh with his knife until no flesh had remained.

And now Sidney Taylor stood again before him, alive and breathing, a grotesquely deformed monstrosity of a man. There he stood, glaring at Eduard with his eyeless black sockets, much like his own empty socket, a jerry can in one hand, a lighter in the other. "What the fuck, you're fucking dead, Taylor! How can you be alive? You were buried! You were fucking *buried! You had a funeral*"

Taylor, ignoring Eduard's hysterical cries, unscrewed the cap of the jerry can, then began to throw a liquid that smelled to Eddie to be petrol, all around the portacabin, on the desk, the floor, the walls.

"What the fuck are you *doing*? You can't be here, I'm *dreaming* this!"

That had to be it. He had received a knock on the head from that big asshole; he was still unconscious, having a nightmare. Dead men don't climb out of their graves. Dead men don't go around burning portacabins. Men with their eyeballs burned out can't even *see*, for fuck's sake!

Taylor began to throw the petrol from the can now over Eddie, soaking his clothes and hair. A splash hit him in the face, stinging his eye, blinding him; he received a mouthful of the foul fluid, which he quickly spat out before coughing uncontrollably. This wasn't real. It *couldn't* be real.

Eduard then heard through his blindness the flicking of a lighter, and two seconds later, his vision went orange, an intense heat suddenly hitting his face. Once the flames had taken hold and the agonising burning of his flesh began, Eduard knew that this was all very real.

NINE

McBride and Jack sat looking at each other in separate corners of the room, both bound at the wrists and ankles. Jack was still gagged, moaning with pain from his broken jaw, whilst McBride's gag had been removed. Drake had placed a heavy-duty torch that resembled a hybrid between a car battery and a car headlight, at one side of the room within the farmhouse in order to provide some light. Drake had seated himself opposite his two prisoners, holding the Glock handgun that he had liberated in one hand, his hip flask in the other. As he stared at McBride, he sipped. McBride stared back, not a trace of fear noticeable on his aged face.

"You know my *name*," he said to his kidnapper, "but do you actually know who I fucking *am?*"

Drake smiled, the old "do you know who you're dealing with here" line. This should be interesting.

"There won't be a place for you to hide now, boy," he continued, "do you know what happens to men that fuck with me?"

"They usually have their faces removed with fire." Drake smiled calmly, taking another sip of his scotch.

McBride's face, bruised and bloody from the beating administered to him by Drake, appeared mildly surprised.

"So, you do know a little about me, then, boy. And yet you're still dumb enough to go toe to toe with me in my own office, in front of my employees."

Employees. That's how he described his thugs. Employees. This man actually thinks of himself as a legitimate businessman. Interesting.

"That's cute."

"Cute? Fucking cute? Boy, I'm going to murder everyone that you fucking care about!"

McBride's face had begun to redden with anger, small flecks of spit flying from his mouth as he spoke.

"That's cute. But the only people that I've ever given a fuck about are already dead. One of them, I killed myself."

McBride glared at him for a few moments, teeth bared, eyes wide. A look that, Drake was sure, would have been frightening and intimidating for many. Drake, however, simply found the angry old face comical.

He continued to stare at the old kingpin, a slight half-smile playing at the corner of his lips as he watched McBride's anger gradually appear to subside, his face transforming from one of rage to one of calm.

"You're not afraid of me, are you?"

To that question, Drake laughed aloud in genuine mirth. Of all the terrors that he had faced throughout his life, encountering this skinny pensioner, gangland boss or not, was not an incident that he would file under the "frightening" category.

"Afraid? Of *you?* No. No. You think you're a dangerous man, and in many ways, you are. But, old man, there is nothing more fucking dangerous in this world than a desperate man with no family, no friends and nothing to lose."

Drake took another sip of his scotch, the fluid feeling warm and sweet as it coated his throat.

McBride looked pensful.

"Who do you work for? Is it The Blackhearts? The Yardies?"

"I work for myself, old man. I'm not a part of your criminal underworld. I'm kind of a freelancer. A gun for hire, in some ways. But on this occasion, I'm working for myself, and for the first time, not even for a profit."

"Then what do you want from me, hey, boy?" He asked, "I'm guessing that if you wanted me dead, you would have done it already. Is it money you want? Drugs? You'll get nothing from me, you fucking cockroach."

Drake stared absently at the gagged younger man, who was glaring across at him angrily, his rapid breathing causing his shoulders to rise and fall like a piston.

"Can you breathe okay?" He asked him. No response, just more death stares and shallow breaths. Drake shrugged, turning his attention back towards McBride.

"McBride, I forget your first name."

"It's John."

"Okay, John, here's what's going to happen. Myself and your man here are going to go into another room and conduct a little… ritual. That's *his* purpose here. Now, *your* purpose here is entirely different."

Drake paused, took another sip from his hip flask.

"Twenty-three years ago, you killed a man named Sidney Taylor. If I told you the full story, you wouldn't believe me, but what I will say is, somebody wants you dead because of what you did to Taylor. I left a note for this person on the door of your portacabin, explaining that they can find you here. This person is somebody that needs my help."

"So, I'm just *bait?*"

Drake smiled.

"Yes."

Clearly, the fact that he, the great John McBride, drug and firearms kingpin, lord of the criminal underworld, had been snatched from his office by a lone nobody, not because of his own vast importance, but simply as bait, a pawn in some game in which he was merely a small cog.

"Taylor was a fucking nobody. The man didn't even have any friends. Why, two and a half decades later, would somebody be gunning for me over *that* piece of shit? He had no family, he wasn't a part of any organisation, he was a cockroach, he was *nothing!*"

Drake shrugged, indifferent. Whatever McBride decided to believe was his own business.

"Well", replied Drake, "they do say that cockroaches would survive a nuclear war."

"That kid owed me everything," McBride continued, ignoring Drake's off-the-cuff remark, "He was a teenager on the streets. I gave him work. He did some arson jobs for me, back when I was in the MC. He delivered some guns and other odd jobs. The little bastard didn't want to join the club, he just wanted to take the money. He would disappear for a few months, then come back. He was a strange kid; nobody ever knew where he was or what he was doing. He had this emotionless expression, like a shark. It was creepy. It was no big shock when he turned out to be a psycho killer. The mistake he made was killing my punters, affecting my business."

"Your punters were paedophiles, John."

"They were paying customers. Some of them regulars."

"So, you killed the girl. She was fourteen, maybe fifteen; A child."

"She was an employee. I put food on her fucking table. She crossed me."

"She was a child."

"Don't take the moral high ground with me, boy. You, me, Taylor, we're not good guys. We do what we need to do to bring home the bacon. We look after number one. Don't think you're better than me, boy. Taylor was no better. He didn't want to rescue that kid, or he would have taken her and got her out of there. But what did he do? He allowed her to keep bringing in the punters, so that he could steal their money. He left her in an unsafe environment, convinced her to betray me, knowing of my reputation. At least under my employment, she had my protection. Nobody would have *dared* to hurt her, not severely, anyway, knowing that they would have *me* to answer to. Taylor caused her death, for his own purposes. He was a fucking shit, and I *personally* killed that double-crossing bastard."

Drake studied McBride's face. Some parts of what he was saying was true; Drake himself was no good guy. He had caused Charlie to surrender her body to a psychopathic killer, and she was now a killer herself, looking at a life sentence. He had killed many men over the years, not necessarily *good* men, but still living, breathing human beings, with grieving mothers and wives, maybe even children.

But you've never pimped out or murdered a child, Drakey boy. We were badasses, but this man is another level, he's fucking evil.

"John, you allowed paedophiles to fuck a child. How much money did you make each time? Was it worth it? You have income from so many other sources, did you *need* that money? Was it worth ruining a kid's *life*? Do you have kids of your own, John?"

McBride turned his face away, breaking eye contact. A sore point, perhaps.

"Besides, John, I'm not here to argue with you about morality. You're right, I'm a bad man. I don't give a shit about you or your *employee* here. Like you said, I'm here for my own purposes. I've done a lot of very bad things in my lifetime, and I'm now doing something to try to redeem myself for at least some of those acts. If that means that I need to throw a horrible bastard of a man to the wolves, a man who sells the innocence of children, then I'm fine with that."

Drake stood, walking towards McBride. It was time for the ritual.

"So, what happens to me when this person arrives, this man who wants me dead? Are you just going to let him have me?"

Drake ignored the question, sitting himself down in front of the aged biker. He held out his hip flask, placing it to McBride's lips. The old man gulped gratefully as Drake poured the golden fluid into his mouth. Drake then reached out with his free hand and patted him twice, affectionately on the shoulder. This man was evil, yes. Deserved to die, certainly. But the older in age that Drake grew, the more he would think about the men that he hurt, how they had ever come to be the way that they were. He imagined them as children, thinking that if perhaps they had received the correct guidance, had good parenting, the right nurturing, they could potentially have grown into good men. McBride was no different. He wasn't born evil, or at least Drake didn't think so, but no doubt, the evil had been kicked into him as a child. He knew that in his own childhood, if not for the dangerous cocktail of an alcoholic father and a sexual predator of an uncle, he himself would certainly have become a better man, or at the very least, a less violent man.

Drake stood, then approached the other, broken-jawed younger man, who was still fixing his eyes upon Drake with an enraged stare.

It was time for the ritual.

The two men, Drake and Jack, sat together in the darkness, cross-legged, facing each other. Jack, the prisoner, remained in restraints, the gag still around his mouth. Drake had secured the cable ties around his wrists to the restraints on his ankles and then had placed the skull into the man's hand. A knife that had belonged to Frank was placed between their legs; despite the fact that Jack was trussed up securely, Drake kept the Glock clutched in his right hand, placed upon his own lap, his left hand was placed over the hand of the other man, securing the skull in place. Drake had told Jack to breathe deeply, close his eyes and clear his mind. He had also told Jack in no uncertain terms that if he tried anything sudden, he would have his brains shot out through the back of his head. A man like this neat-looking fellow, working for an organisation dealing in human trafficking and child prostitution, was exactly the type of man that Drake had sought all along; immoral, living in the shadows and on the edges of society. A man whose life expectancy was short, a man whose disappearance would not be investigated too thoroughly by the authorities, a man with many potential enemies, a man that deserved, more than most at least, whatever was coming to him. Of course, John McBride deserved a worse fate, however Frankie wouldn't appreciate a host body so old and decrepit. Besides, there were other forces at play that had very different plans for the old man; Drake was not planning to get in the way of that. He had his plan in mind, he would finally set right some of the wrongs that he had committed.

Jack continued to stare at Drake with a malevolent stare that he had probably practiced in a mirror; his intimidating look.

That's cute.

Drake smiled, chuckling to himself softly.

"Listen, son," he said, "that wide-eyed glare doesn't intimidate me. If you hadn't noticed, I showed up at your boss's office unarmed and took on four of you. Now I have two of you prisoner, including the big kingpin who is sat tied up in the next room pissing his pants. Now, if you don't do as I say and start meditating, and doing it properly, I may just put a fucking hole in your head then drag your boss in here instead. It makes not the slightest bit of difference to me. It's your call, son."

Jack continued with his soul-burning stare, seemingly unphased by Drake's warning. Drake shrugged, then raised the pistol until it was level with Jack's face. He held it there for a second, before Jack sighed, dropping his gaze down to the floor, defeated, all traces of fight drained from his expression.

That's what I thought.

Drake lifted his hand from the other man's hand holding the skull, and carefully pulled the gag down, over the chin and revealing his mouth. Jack gasped in pain; his jaw was immensely swollen.

"What's your name, son?"

"Hack." He answered, through his inflamed mouth.

"That's Jack, I'm guessing. I think John next door said you were called Jack."

Drake produced his hip flask, and, as he had done with McBride, placed the bottle against Jack's lips, pouring the scotch into his mouth, which he accepted, desperately swallowing the liquor with great zeal. Drake allowed the younger man to finish the bottle, recognising that Jack was in pain. Pain that *he* had caused. Once the flask had been drained, Drake reached over and patted Jack's shoulder twice.

Jack appeared visibly refreshed by the whisky, however he was still clearly in great discomfort.

"Listen Jack, I'll be honest with you. I'm not going to kill you, but your body is going to be offered as a *vessel*. We are going to be contacting the dead."

Jack looked up at Drake, studying his face; his expression appeared to be a hybrid of confusion and mild amusement.

He thinks I'm nuts.

"I know you think I'm a basket case, kid. Maybe I am. Just *humour* me, please."

Jack looked away, frowning, then turned back towards Drake, still baffled. He shrugged. Drake placed his hand back onto Jack's, squeezing it affectionately. This poor kid; he had fallen in with the wrong crowd, certainly. He had probably done some very bad things. Still, no matter what atrocities that Drake attempted to conjure in his mind and attribute to this swollen-jawed young man, he still felt the guilt deep within his gut.

"Okay Jack," said Drake, "start breathing. Clear your mind. I know it's been a rough day for you, but we need to do this before my guest arrives."

They began.

Drake's stomach began to flutter with the familiar, fearful sensation that always accompanied his consultations with the skull. These consultations had become to Drake one of the very few incidents in his life that caused the feeling of fear within him; he no longer felt any dread in firefights or brawls, he had no phobias that he could think of. The skull, and the memory of his departed uncle, were the only two things in his life with the capability to instil terror within him.

The two men breathed deeply, down into the pits of their stomachs, slowly. Long breaths, drawing in the oxygen through their nostrils, filling their lungs, then back out through their mouths. Their heart rates slowed as they did so; Drake finding his body relaxing despite his nerves, his mind and body calming themselves as the skull began to radiate its heat, warming his hand, causing the familiar pins and needles.

Their breathing unconsciously fell into synchronisation, their bellies rising and falling in unison as they fell deeper into trance.

Their breaths went in, then out.

In, then out.

In, out.

In.

Out.

In.

Out.

The rain hammered down onto his head, trickling down over his face, soaking into his beard. Drake could see the outlines of trees in the darkness, in a landscape that seemed familiar.

Before him, in the shadows, he could distinguish the silhouette of a powerfully-built man, with a shovel, throwing shovelfuls of dirt into something that could not be seen through the limited ambient light, but what Drake had guessed to be a hole in the ground.

The shape of the man patted down the hole he had covered using his shovel, before standing upright, as though in a military attention stance, and then, chin raised high, he began to sing.

"La Legion marche vers le front,

En chantant nous suivons,

Heritiers de ses traditions,

Nous sommes avec elle…"

The Regimental song. This man was a Legionnaire.

He is a Legionnaire. That's me. That's me burying Frank.

Drake turned away from the scene, not wishing to again relive that harrowing moment, the worst deed that he had ever committed. Of all the men that he had killed or hurt, murdering Frank, the man that had been his life companion, his brother, had stung the deepest. That singular act, he knew, was one that he would never fully recover from, or forgive himself for.

As his head turned away from the scene, his peripheral vision caught sight of something out of the ordinary; humanoid shapes, tall and thin, at the corner of his left eye. He turned his head, squinting his eyes to focus. There stood two men, tall and thin, wraithlike. Drake stepped towards them, studying their faces in the darkness through the rain. He wiped his sleeve across his eyes, clearing away the moisture, squinted again, stepped another pace forwards, and stopped. He knew these men, both of them.

Before him stood the tall, wiry bald-headed Aayush, the man that he and Frank had befriended whilst serving time in Tihar prison. Next to him stood the milky-eyed old shaman, Naja Haje.

How could he be there watching Frank's funeral? Frank had killed him.

Drake stared at Naja Haje for several seconds.

Is it him? Could Drake be mistaken? Was Naja actually there at the burial? Or was something fucking with his head?

As Drake stared at the two men in confusion, he again caught sight, with his peripheral vision, of something else unnatural to the surroundings. Again, a human shape standing close, over his shoulder. He turned, alarmed, and started in fear, his breath catching in his throat. Drake stumbled backwards, feeling the overwhelming urge to cry out loud, and yet his voice failed him.

Pongo the clown grinned at him in the darkness, rotting teeth baring out from between painted red lips, his curly green hair sodden with rain. The clown's bony, oversized hand reached out towards Drake, down towards his groin.

Then, he was back in the room. The farmhouse, damp and familiar, with the silhouette of Jack sat facing him, his shoulders rising and falling slowly as he breathed steadily. Drake closed his eyes, focusing again on clarity of the mind, and on the task at hand. Frank was relying on him. Drake drew in a long, slow breath.

"Hey, Drakey boy." A voice whispered in the darkness.

Frank.

Drake's eyes snapped open, his heart pounding against his ribs.

"Frank?"

Jack's face looked back at him, his smile deformed by the swelling around his face. Jack's face, but *different* somehow. The narrow-eyed squint, the half-smile, the defiant expression with an air of superiority.

Frank.

"How you doing, brother?"

Drake placed his hands upon Jack's shoulders (Frank's shoulders?) and placed his forehead against the other man's, exhaling a long, relieved breath. His brother. Frank. He had done it. Frank was home, by his side again. His partner, his sidekick, his only friend.

"Frank, I've got you back. I've got you back." Drake's shaky voice was racked with emotion. He sobbed once, before catching himself, controlling his breathing, calming his heart.

"How about you cut these bonds, Drakey?"

"Of course." Drake fumbled in the darkness for Frank's knife, opening the blade and quickly cutting away the cable ties that restrained his long-lost companion.

Frank rubbed his wrists, again bringing back some circulation into his hands.

"What's wrong with my jaw, Drakey? Did you have to rough up this guy? Who is he, anyhow?"

"He's some thug from McBride's crew. Remember McBride?"

Frank looked up in surprise.

"You're fucking with McBride's crew?"

"Well McBride himself is tied up in the next room, if that answers your question."

Frank laughed out loud.

"Fuck in hell, Drakey. Keeping up the badass reputation in my absence, buddy. I like it."

"Well you're not absent anymore, Frankie. You can get some beers inside you soon."

Frank fell silent, shaking his head sadly.

"What, Frank? I've brought you back. You can *live* again."

"No, Drakey. I'm not staying. I can't."

Drake looked into Frank's eyes, questioningly, a pained expression painted on his brow.

"What do you mean, Frankie?" he asked, "I've thought of nothing for these past years but bringing you back. My entire life has revolved around this."

"Well now you can move on, Drakey." Frank smiled sadly, "There's more to this existence than the limitations of this physical world, Ash. Our travels will continue together. I'll be waiting. Get rid of that fucking skull. It's a cancer. Just bury it here on this land and walk away. Or smash the thing. Just get as far away from it as possible. There are dark things that follow it; I'm not talking the spirits of dead folk, I mean ancient things, things that have never even been human. They've been on this world longer than man, they feed on fear, on pain, and especially on death. You've seen your uncle, I know that. That wasn't him, Ash. That was something much worse. Wherever you go, it will be there, until you get that skull out of your life. It will claim your life eventually, like it took mine, unless you get rid of it. Break the chain."

"No, Frank, it was *me* that took your life."

"It *made* you do it, Ash. I was already gone, past the point of no return. I couldn't have come back, it had latched itself on too deep, like a tick. These things are parasites. You did the world a service by killing it. If that thing had gotten out of that forest, using my body, it would have done unspeakable things. You don't need to feel guilt anymore. I was the one that wanted the skull, I instigated all of this. All you did was kill something fucking evil, and in doing so, you set me free."

Drake gripped Frank's shoulder, squeezing it tightly.

"You can *live* again, Frank. You can *stay*."

"I can't. A human soul can only hold onto a body for limited periods. If a soul is *really* desperate, angry, with unfinished business, sometimes it can cling on for a little longer, but it's draining, exhausting. It would be like constantly trying to climb up a greased rope. I need to let go, Ash. Let this kid have his body back and walk away from this. This poor kid didn't ask for any of this."

Drake wiped a tear from his cheek with his sleeve.

Don't let Frank see me weep.

"Since when did you grow a conscience, Frankie?" Drake smiled.

"Just try to do the right thing, Ash. Please."

"Frankie, there's something that I wanted to say to you, on the night that you died."

"I know, Ash. You don't need to say it."

"It's important, Frank."

Silence. The sound of the slow inhalations and exhalations, the creaking of the old building, the wind whistling steadily through the empty windows, but not a whisper from the voice of Frank.

"Frank?"

Jack had his eyes closed, lost in trance. Sleeping peacefully, seemingly blissfully unaware of the fact that his body had just seconds before been host to a dead man.

"Goodbye, Frank. We'll meet again, brother."

McBride had managed to slide himself across to the doorway, to the rough, exposed brick edge where the wooden frame had long since rotted away. He raised his hands, placing the thick cable tie against the jagged corner, then, moving his arms up and down in a saw-like motion, he began to wear away the plastic.

The plan, he decided, would be not to directly engage his enemy at this stage; his kidnapper had the firearm, his large size and his relative youth to his advantage. McBride thought that at this moment, the best plan of attack would be to slip away silently, then to return with reinforcements; he would burn this wreck of a farmhouse down if he had to. That prick was going to fry, one way or the other.

The bond wore through after a minute or so of grinding the cable tie hard against the brick, and McBride pulled his hands apart, shaking them off, clenching and unclenching his fingers, feeling the blood rushing back to the tips. Hands done, now for the awkward part, the ankles. The plastic was an inch wide, strong and thick. He wasn't going to be able to snap it using brute force, and to attempt to scrape it against the brick would be too awkward, physically. McBride checked his pockets, looking for keys, his pocketknife, anything to aid in his escape; the big guy had emptied them all, even taken his wallet. *Thieving bastard.*

McBride rested himself for a moment, placing his back against the cold wall, re-evaluating his options. He could hop down the stairs, maybe crawl.

Then what? Hop back to town?

Frustrated, he pulled his knees apart, trying in vain to stretch out the thick, strong plastic, merely causing himself pain to the ankles.

The stranger had said that there would be someone coming, someone looking for revenge against him for his murder of a nobody, a loner, way back in the mid-nineties. Sidney Taylor had no real friends; Taylor was a drifter, wandering from town to town making his crust any way that he could. He had no roots whatsoever. Taylor had been an orphan without any known siblings, fleeing his orphanage in his mid-teens. McBride had employed the kid, in a way. He had caught him attempting to steal a bike from a fellow Blackheart, and himself and two others had run over to the kid to give him a beating, but to McBride's surprise, the boy had put up a good fight, knocking down himself and one other. Laughing at this young boy's ferociousness, McBride had calmed him down by offering him food and beer, taking him inside for a plate of fried chicken and a few bottles of lager. He offered young Sidney a room in one of his properties, and cash in exchange for occasional taskings, such as burning a car or bike here or there, setting a rival clubhouse alight, delivering a few packages to his customers. This had continued for a few months, until the lad had disappeared without a word. He re-emerged just over a year later, asking McBride if there was any work that he needed doing. Then, after a few weeks, he vanished away again. This pattern continued for several years, with Taylor sometimes staying around for only a few days, sometimes several months. The work that McBride tasked him with evolved over the years, from petty arson and deliveries to enforcer roles; Sid often went out to rough up someone that owed money, broke somebody's legs or arm or whatever was required. He never did seem keen on this type of work, which was surprising, especially since later, all the bodies were discovered, victims of Taylor, yet the young man begrudgingly would carry out some enforcement work if required, before eventually wandering away to drift yet again. Sidney Taylor was an absolute mystery. Perhaps he had made friends during his travels, his time away from Thornham. Taylor, however, was not a man that possessed any social skills to speak of; when the lad had gotten himself shacked up with a pretty barmaid, McBride had been mildly shocked, and yet when they had discovered the bodies and suspected Taylor, McBride had not been surprised in the slightest. The Psychotic bastard had not only killed eighteen of McBride's customers, which, in itself, would warrant severe punishment, but Taylor had also butchered two of McBride's officers that had visited the farmhouse to solve the problem. Two of his best men. This warranted McBride's personal attention, as well as his signature execution. Normally, this type of insult would warrant the target's family to be wiped out as an example, a deterrent to anyone else that felt that they could try their luck by testing McBride's patience; Sidney Taylor, however, had no family. Therefore, the barmaid had been on that occasion the only collateral damage in the hit.

Of the six men that went to the barmaid's flat that night, the only current survivors were himself and Eduard. And Eddie, of course, had been left back at the office, packaged up like a gift for whoever was on the warpath seeking to avenge Taylor. McBride assumed that whoever it was that wanted him dead, would also be looking for Eddie. Walters had been killed that week, in his own flat, in a hit that McBride had assumed at the time was a personal beef; Walters tended to rub folk up the wrong way, fucked a lot of married women, didn't pay back his debts, but now, McBride knew the truth; Sidney Taylor's avenging angel was rubbing them all out. Kuklinski, who had also assisted in the killing of Taylor, had been found dead shortly after the event after a home invasion during which nothing obvious had been stolen. His girlfriend at the time, a lap dancer who had been working in the strip club at the time of Kuklinski's death, had said that the only item that appeared to be missing was an odd skull that he had acquired from somewhere and placed atop the television, an ornament that she described as "ugly", claiming that it had been creeping her out ever since he had brought the thing home.

And now, it seemed, McBride may be the only living survivor of that bloody night, assuming that their hunter had looked for them at the office first; and there he was, bound by the ankles, unable to flee, and unarmed.

Come on, John, you've been in much worse scrapes than this. You're a survivor. Now get out of that fucking cable tie.

With that thought in mind, and with a new burst of enthusiasm, McBride began to crawl towards the exit, pulling himself forwards with his hands, then bringing his knees up to his chest, dragging his knees across the rough, grimy floor, then repeating. Perhaps there would be a sharp rock outside, or a shard of glass, a primitive tool with which to free himself. There were bottles strewn around the room, sure, but breaking one would surely alert the big bastard in the next room. Outside, there would be something to use. Staying inside the building and wallowing in self-pity was not only not an option; it just wasn't John McBride. He was going to get out, gather some men, some real horrible bastards, and then… there would be blood.

Trying to ignore the pain on his knees, McBride dragged himself closer to the exit, seeing the light at the end of the tunnel in the form of the rotting, worm and louse-ridden wood that formed the exit, and potential freedom beyond.

He was within a couple of metres of the exit, when what remained of the door creaked open on its rusted hinges and a large silhouette filled the frame; a muscular, thick-haired man whose features could not be seen against the backdrop of ambient moonlight. At first glance, McBride thought the figure to be his kidnapper, being of similar height and build, however the hair was different, and besides, he was still in the next room with Jack, doing whatever it was that he was doing.

McBride stopped in his tracks, on his knees like a dog, with grey streaks of hair hanging down over his face, looking up in surprise at the giant towering over him.

"Who the fuck *are* you?" He asked. "why do you even give a crap about Sidney Taylor? He was nothing! Do you really want to fuck with a man like *me* over a loser like *him*?"

The man stepped forwards, revealing, in the dim light that streamed in from the empty hole that had once been a window, a small glimpse of his face. What McBride saw, there in the darkness, caused him to clench his teeth tightly in terror as he froze to the spot, unable to move, unable to speak. His breath caught in his throat, his neck hairs stood on end.

It was Taylor. Sidney Taylor. Not only was it Sidney Taylor, but before his eyes stood Sidney Taylor looking exactly as McBride had left him; faceless, eyeless, with a scorched, smoking skull.

TEN

Shaking his hip flask, Drake sighed. Empty. He had not even been given the chance to have one final drink with Frank, and now he was gone, returned to whatever plane of existence that it was where he now resided. Drake now understood that Frank's death had not been his fault, a fact that had freed him in so many ways; what was now happening to Charlie, however, was entirely his fault, and was his burden to bear.

Drake looked down at Jack, still deep in trance, then turned and walked towards the door to the next room. McBride seemed to Drake to be a wily old bastard, no doubt that by now the old crime lord would have attempted to wriggle his way off the property and to his freedom, plotting in his mind Drake's demise, like the coyote from the roadrunner cartoons, scheming to catch that bird.

Under ordinary circumstances, Drake would never harm a man as elderly as McBride, however, for a human trafficker and head of a child prostitution ring, he had made an exception. True, Drake himself was more of a Satan than a Saint Peter, but to harm a child was a line, in Drake's and indeed also even in Franks book, that should never be crossed. Giving an old man a kicking was a cowardly act, but when that man was John McBride, Drake didn't feel that he would be losing any sleep over it.

He stepped through the doorway into the large room beyond, scanning the darkness for McBride. There were two lines of moonlight, one from the open door, another from the glassless window, throwing limited illumination across the far side of the room. Drake heard McBride before he saw him, wheezing desperately, almost as though the old man were suffering a heart attack. He saw him then, lying on the ground on his side, his face a mask of pure terror, teeth bared, eyes wide, staring beyond Drake, at something in the dark corner, to Drake's left, something that had turned this tough old biker into a gibbering wreck of a man.

Drake felt the presence then, in the corner to his left, a presence that caused his hair to stand on end. He slowly turned his head, seeing a large shape, a figure in the darkness, as still as death.

Sidney.

Drake stepped away from the figure, keeping his eyes fixed upon it, raising his hands, still holding the Glock, in a gesture of peace. He didn't want to fight this thing; he didn't want to hurt Charlie, and besides, Sidney Taylor was not his enemy tonight.

"Sidney," he said, calmly, "I know who you are, and I know why you're here. I'm not here to stop you. I brought McBride here for you."

The figure, unmoving, remained silent. Drake could see that something about its face was wrong, inhuman somehow.

"You have a conscience, Sid, I know that," he continued, taking another step backwards, "you took that young girl under your wing. You avenged her death."

Drake knew that what he was saying was largely romanticising the actions of the sinister figure before him; it was far more likely that this spectral killer had once seen the girl as a financial opportunity, killing her punters in order to steal their money, his delivery of "vengeance" more a matter of self-preservation than a one of sentimental anger over her death. This was not the time, however, to be throwing rocks at the hornet's nest, and besides, the men that he did murder, men who took advantage of an exploited child, really did deserve his blade.

"Just think of the girl whose body you have taken," Drake continued, "I know that you need to avenge yourself, and avenge Nicola.."

Hearing that name, the shape stirred, rising taller, tensing. A soft hissing noise was heard, causing McBride's breathing to hasten, growing louder as the old man began to panic.

"All I'm asking for, Sid, is that once you're done here, leave her, leave the mortal world. Go and be with Nicola. Be at peace, Sid. Your business is finished. And the man in the next room, he's not involved. He's too young. Give him a break, please."

With that, Drake crept away from the figure, walking slowly backwards, hands raised, towards the exit, never taking his sight away from the shape in the corner. As he passed through the door, the room suddenly began to glow bright as a blast of fire flew from the hand of the dark figure, illuminating the dark corners. He was holding a blowtorch. Before Drake passed through the door and out of the building, he saw, standing silently in the corner opposite from Sid, two more spectral figures, spectators. One of them was a teenage girl, the other a young woman. They stared blankly down at McBride, waiting patiently to witness the act that would complete their own unfinished business, and free their tormented souls. Both of these apparitions appeared to have had had their throats cut, with blood stains running down from their necks, staining their clothing. The last vision in Drake's eyes before exiting that building was that faceless, scorched skull as it crept towards McBride, clutching its blowtorch.

Enjoy yourself, Sid.

Drake walked across to his van to retrieve a bottle of Macallan scotch from a bag in the rear; a bottle that he had paid a steep price for and saved for his reunion with Frank. Tonight had been that reunion, as brief as it had been, and although it was unfortunate that Frank had not been able to taste it and share the moment with him, he did sense in the air the big dumb bastard's presence.

I'm here, Drakey boy. I always have been. I told you I'll be waiting. We have so much more to see.

Within the farmhouse, McBride was letting out the most piercing, blood curdling screams, shouting in tongues, the babbling of pure agony and mind-numbing terror.

Karma, in the form of a dead serial killer with a blowtorch. How strange life is.

Taking a sip straight from the bottle, Drake rinsed his mouth with the thirty-year old scotch. It tasted of heaven. He then poured a dram of the golden liquid out onto the ground, then raised the bottle high into the air.

"Frank," he said, holding the bottle high and toasting his brother, "Honneur et Fidelitie." The moon was full. Frank had always loved gazing at the moon, dating right back to their first camping trip, their first beer. Drake smiled fondly at the memory, retrieving, from his side pocket, the small photo album. He flicked to the first page, himself and Frank, aged twenty-two, having just completed their parachutist course within the second foreign parachute regiment, freshly badged, fresh faced. Frank had been so proud of his parachute badge, so proud that he had worn the metal badge on his civilian jacket for several weeks after earning it, until the point that the other boys in the unit had begun to laugh about it. He always did love achieving such little tokens. He had been the same when the two of them had earned their commando brevets, or their Brazilian Jiu Jitsu black belts, although Frank had earned his belt a good eight months before Drake.

You were always better than me, Frank, in every way. I was a stronger man just by trying to be more like you.

The screams within the walls continued. Taylor was taking his time. Drake sipped at his Macallan, easily the best whisky that he had ever tasted.

For the price, I'd hope so.

As he drank, he looked across at the scenery; the moonlit trees and fields looked beautiful, serene. It was hard to piece together the calm, eye-catching landscape with the horrors that were currently occurring within the decrepit old building behind him, far from where anyone could hear the screams of pain and fear. As he gazed amongst the trees, he saw, in a small wood block twenty metres or so away, two tall, thin figures, standing, quietly watching the farmhouse and listening to the agonised wailing within.

Drake recalled the vision of himself burying Frank, the image of the two wraithlike men watching the events unfold from the darkness of the trees.

Naja Haje and Aayush.

From that moment, Drake understood. He knew how to undo what he had created.

After the screaming had finally stopped, and the glow of the blowtorch from behind the door had subsided, Drake decided to enter the building again. Inside, Charlie sat, alone and wide-eyed, with her back to the rear wall, staring across the floor at the corpse of McBride; his face a smouldering, blackened skull. The blowtorch had been tossed aside, lying on its side a couple of metres away from the body.

Drake firstly approached Charlie, who looked up at Drake as he approached, recognition registering in her frightened eyes. He sat himself beside her, then handed her the Macallan bottle. She snatched the bottle, gulping big mouthfuls of the stuff like a dehydrated woman with a bottle of ice water. Ash patted her on the shoulder as she drank. Once she had removed the bottle from her lips, she turned towards him, embracing him tightly. Drake was mildly surprised, as he had actually expected a slap to the face rather than a warm embrace, but nonetheless, he hugged her back, ruffling her hair. This girl had been through so much shit because of him; it was time to put it right. Drake gently pulled Charlie's arms away, looking into her eyes.

"I'm sorry, Charlie," he said, "this was all my fault. I'm going to make things better now, to the best of my ability."

Charlie stared once more at the blackened skull face of McBride before her, her eyes full of terror. This poor girl would never forget that burned skull, Drake knew that. It would be with her, in the darkness, in her dreams.

"Sid did that, didn't he?"

"Yes, he did."

"Did you see him?"

"Yes, I did."

"He didn't try to hurt you?"

"No. He was only here for John McBride."

Charlie for a few moments went deep into thought, studying the laces of her boots.

"You know, when Sid died, he didn't scream. They burned away his skin and his eyes, and he just took it quietly. Not a whimper. The only sound that he made was, before they burned away his lips, to tell them that they would see him again. He knew he would be coming back."

"Did you see that?"

"I saw everything. I saw his whole life. Did you know that he used to own that skull of yours?"

Drake looked at her, startled. Sidney Taylor owned the skull?

"Well," he said, "I guess that makes sense. A trail of blood follows that bastard thing wherever it goes."

Drake stood and ruffled Charlie's hair. He told her that he would be back in a few seconds, then he walked into the next room. Jack was seated on the floor, shivering in the cold, hugging his knees. How much of the horrors in the next room he had witnessed, Drake was unsure, but he would have certainly heard the blood-curdling screams and smelt the burning flesh, no doubt terrified that he was going to be next.

"Jack, it's over, kid." Drake said. "There's a girl next door, she will give you a lift into town shortly. You can go home again."

Drake walked over to the huddled, frightened figure, holding out the bottle. Jack accepted it with a trembling hand, then Drake walked over to the centre of the room, retrieving the skull from the floor. Then, carrying the skull in his fist, he walked back through the doorway into the larger room, towards the blowtorch.

He placed the skull into his inside jacket pocket, then knelt before the blowtorch, picking it up. Then, with his sleeve, Drake wiped the handle, clearing away Charlie's prints, before grasping it tightly, leaving his fingerprints and DNA behind, then placing it back onto the floor. He then approached Charlie.

"Do you have the knife?"

Charlie frowned, for a moment not understanding, then, with a flash of recognition in her eyes, she pulled out a folding knife from within her inside pocket, and threw it to Drake, who caught it in one hand. Again, he wiped down the handle before placing his own prints all over it.

Drake then sat back down, beside her, closing his eyes. A moment to compose himself before carrying out the inevitable act.

"What did I do, Ash?" Charlie asked, "did I do *that*?" She pointed towards the burned skull face in the centre of the room, "I mean, I know it was Sid, but it was also me, wasn't it? It was my body, my hands."

"No," Drake replied, "*I* did it. Always remember that, and don't ever change your story." Drake pulled a piece of paper from his jeans pocket, handing it to Charlie, the note that he had written whilst he had been sitting in the van listening to McBride's face being painfully removed.

"In there is a confession. I killed Frank Jackson in Chile. The note says that Frank wasn't himself, he had some kind of fever and he attacked me. I killed him in self-defence. I could never live with it; not a day went by that I didn't think of it. In that note is also a confession to the murders of McBride and Walters. The man at the office that ran away, if he speaks to anyone, will give my description and explain that I attacked Jack before he did a runner. Jack in there, if he talks, won't give your description because he didn't see you do anything. He'll describe me, and possibly a big guy with a burned off face. Nobody will take that seriously. I've explained in the note that McBride took away my livelihood when he took over the security industry in the area, which is why I went after him. I've also explained that you weren't involved, you were scared and waiting in the van when I killed these guys."

Charlie looked at him, not quite understanding.

"Ash, why are you doing this?"

"I caused this, Charlie. Too many lives have been ruined because of me. I need Frank's mother to know the truth, and I need you to be able to get on with your life."

Reaching into his jeans pocket, Drake handed Charlie his van keys.

"Take yourself and the young guy in the next room into town. There is around ten grand in cash in one of the bags in the back of the van. I explained in the note that the van is yours. Whatever legal weight that may hold, I don't know, but keep the cash. It should help set you up with a place to live. Go back to school, Charlie. Get a part-time job, but also get yourself qualified for something better. You're smart. You're better than bar work."

Drake stood, stretching out his arms.

"I've had a good run. I've travelled the world, I've seen and done more than most would in ten lifetimes. Now, it's time for the next chapter in my story."

Charlie climbed to her feet, wobbling slightly on one leg, ridden with terrible pins and needles.

"What are you doing, Ash? I don't understand."

Drake ignored her question, reaching into the back of his jeans, pulling out the Glock handgun that had been tucked there. With his other hand, he retrieved the skull from his jacket pocket. With these two objects in hand, he walked out into the moonlight, head held high, shoulders back, standing proud.

Charlie followed him, grabbed his shoulders from behind.

"Ash, please.." she sobbed, sensing that he was about to disappear from her life, not wanting him to. Despite the danger that he had exposed her to, he had remained loyal to her, made sure that she was okay, and set everything right again. She felt safe around him, a feeling that she had never felt around anybody else.

"Charlie, I have to do this."

Then she saw the two tall, thin figures. They were standing only a few metres away, watching Ash, waiting. One of them she recognised, from the vision during her blackout. *Aayush.*

"Charlie, I'm just going to ask one thing of you. *Don't touch that fucking skull.*"

I'm waiting for you, Drakey boy.

Standing tall, chin high, Drake then began to sing.

"La Legion marche vers le front,
En chantant nous suivons,
Heritiers de ses traditions,
Nous sommes avec elle…"

With that, he lifted the Glock, placed it against the side of his head, and pulled the trigger. Dark matter exploded from the opposite side of his head with a loud crack, and Charlie screamed, watching as Ash fell to his knees, then forwards, onto his face into the wet grass. The skull rolled across the ground, flecks of Drake's blood spattered across the surface.

Charlie fell to her knees, sobbing uncontrollably, hugging the big man's corpse.

"You were a good man Ash, you were. You didn't think you were, but you had a big heart. You were the best man I ever met." She whispered into his ear, between sobs.

Aayush had approached, bending slowly to pick up the skull. He carried the relic back over to his milky-eyed companion and handed it to him, before the two of them turned to walk away, into the trees.

From a rack of newspapers in a local newsagents, she saw him for the first time. A rugged, scarred man, wearing body armour and Oakley wrap-around shades, holding an assault rifle in an unidentified desert. Claire had never felt an attraction to any of the usual losers from school, the gelled hair, the skinny jeans, they all looked more like women these days. This guy in the picture, now *that* was a real man. The article beside the picture explained how this man had single-handedly hunted down an underworld kingpin, killing him and his henchmen before blowing out his own brains. Apparently, he had killed the kingpin with a blowtorch, a signature torture and execution method thought to have been used by the gangland boss himself, against his own enemies. This man, Ashton Drake, ex-legionnaire and mercenary, was a real-life action hero. A *real* man. Claire stuffed the newspaper discreetly into her satchel. That article, she would cut out and keep. Then, from the solitude of her room, she would google search this man on her tablet. Finally, she had found someone worthy of her interest. It was a terrible shame that the man was dead.

Two years had passed since Drake's passing at that cursed farmhouse. Charlie had taken the van, and the money, as he had instructed, setting herself up in a new room and returning to college. Ash's final words to Charlie had been wise; she really had been wasting her life pulling pints and living in one cockroach-infested bedsit after another. Charlie had begun her studies of media, journalism and communication the following

September following Ash's death, whilst working part time in the same bar that Sidney Taylor had met his one love, Nicola Donovan. There were still the naysayers who would insist that Sidney had used Nicola simply as a means to hide from his aggressors, that he cared nothing of young Susie whose customers he had butchered, but no. Charlie had shared her body with the very man's essence, his soul. She had felt his pain, his regrets over how his actions had indirectly led to the deaths of the only two people that he had ever cared for. Using her free time to talk to the townsfolk, visit the family members of Nicola and spend real time around Thornham getting to know the real Sidney Taylor, the real Nicola Donovan, Charlie knew that *her* book on the legend of Sid would really do him justice, and show the world that Nicola and young Susie were much more than mere pawns in the story, were not simply used by the deceased killer as a means to an end. Of course, Ash would receive his own chapter in the book, after all, he was a part of the legend, and brought about the closure of the saga. Ash, who delivered justice to those men who had ended the lives of Sid, along with the two girls that he had cared for, right there in that same farmhouse around which the entire story had centred. She wouldn't glorify his actions; he wouldn't have liked that.

Nicola Donovan's family had been overwhelmed at Charlie's interest in their daughter, happy in the knowledge that her book would detail at length the life of Nicola, who, for most journalists, was portrayed as nothing but another victim, a name, a small photograph, nothing more. Nicola's mother knew the deep love that the young couple had shared, and whilst she could never forgive Sidney for bringing those wolves to the door that had taken her Nicola away, she knew that her daughter would have wanted her true story to be told; she would not have wanted to be seen as some bimbo who was foolish enough to have been taken in by a man who cared nothing for her and wanted nothing more than the sanctuary that her home could offer. The Donovan family had given Charlie some photographs of Sidney and Nicola, photographs never before shown to the press, for which Charlie was grateful.

One of these photographs, portraying a picture of Sidney, unsmiling with deep sadness in his eyes, standing behind a smiling Nicola, his arms protectively wrapped around her waist, his chin on her shoulder, she framed, placing next to her framed photo of young Ashton, smiling proudly next to his giant of a friend Frank, both of the young men clad in their combat uniforms and the green berets of their unit in the French Foreign Legion. Charlie often pondered on the pain in Sidney's eyes; the guilt of Susie's death, the knowledge of the blood that he had shed, the sense that his time with his true love would be short. A tragic life, filled with nothing but blood and heartache.

Charlie felt Ash's presence sometimes, there in the room with her. She had quit smoking, almost, and cut down on the booze, sometimes not touching a drop for two weeks at a time, however when the mood became dark, especially when she thought of him and turned to the bottle, she felt him there. She never drank alone. He gave her courage, inspired her, made her want to achieve greater things. She would do him justice. She would tell *his* story.

Staring into the flames of the campfire, he listened to the whispers. The same rumours that had heard being muttered in remote spots all over the world, amongst the same circles of experience seekers, backpacking, like himself, through the most far-flung, uninhabited regions far from the beaten track. Himself and James had begun these journeys originally as a gap year after their first year of University, and yet five years later, had still not returned home. The dull life of s student studying medicine in a mediocre town, after the places they had been, the things they had seen, seemed now somehow unbearable. Especially when they were learning that there was much more to this existence than even modern science had discovered; things that most educated men would not even believe possible even if seeing it with their own eyes; they had seen men levitate, women disappearing into bursts of flame. They had witnessed creatures deep in jungles that were not only undiscovered by man, but that defied physical laws. Medicine somehow now seemed redundant, no longer an enigma. The physical world was no challenge, the spiritual, however, had much more to offer in the way of mystery.

He listened, exhaling the smoke from his joint as he passed it along to James. This man, this tall, thin man whose body appeared to be completely bereft of bodily fat, baring every fibre of sinewy muscle beneath his skin, was speaking of a relic, an ancient relic through which the dead could be not only summoned, but drawn out from hell and placed once more into a physical body. Were the right person to hold this relic, this skull, he claimed, and use it to summon you after your death, then you could return, take a physical form and live again. What was more, he said, this skull, this crystal skull, could bring forth other beings, those that had walked the earth since before the dawn of man, those beings that were not human, not physical, those that the ancients had called many names. They had been called Gods, Angels and Demons amongst countless other names across the languages of the thousands of tribes and civilisations throughout the history of mankind; for some of them, their knowledge was vast, their perceptions of time, space and dimension so *different* and infinitely superior to ours, that were we to see just a tiny fraction of their consciousness, our minds would be shattered.

He listened to the thin man, soaking up every word. This was truly where his life's work should begin. These beings, *Gods*, even, could teach him so much, *show* him so much, that any other pursuit on this earth was meaningless.

"And where, Aayush, my good man," he said, "Could I find such a relic as this skull?"

"There is a shaman, living in isolation in Machu Pichu. His name is Naja Haje."